I WON'T TELL YOU WHAT WAS IN THE MYSTERIOUS PHIAL . . . TO DO SO WOULD BE CRUEL AND INHUMANE PUNISHMENT. BUT I WILL SAY THAT THE NOVEL—AT LEAST ONE FERVENTLY HOPES IT IS A NOVEL—IS A UNIQUE READING EXPERIENCE.

—*Los Angeles Herald Examiner*

. . . Barjavel's skill is in making you want to read on.

—*Newsday*

JEANNE CORBET SPENDS 17 YEARS SEARCHING FOR HER LOVER, ROLAND, WHO DISAPPEARED UNDER MYSTERIOUS CIRCUMSTANCES. WHAT HAPPENED TO HIM AND WHY, AND WHAT HAPPENS TO THEM WHEN THEY MEET AGAIN AFTER BEING APART FOR ALMOST TWO DECADES, WILL KEEP READERS TURNING PAGES UNTIL THE FINAL CHILLING SENTENCE.

—*Minneapolis Tribune*

In this suspense story, the great secret which constitutes the book's raison d'etre is kept long enough to tantalize and to hook the reader.

—*Best Sellers*

A SUSPENSEFUL . . . TALE IN WHICH GENETIC RATHER THAN GALACTIC DISCOVERIES ARE MADE WHEN AN INDIAN BRAHMIN ENGAGED IN BIOLOGICAL RESEARCH ISOLATES A CONTAGIOUS VIRUS . . . TENSION AND ANXIETY ARE MAINTAINED THROUGHOUT . . .

—*ALA Booklist*

Books by René Barjavel

The Immortals
The Ice People

THE
IMMORTALS

by René Barjavel

Translated from the French by Eileen Finletter

BALLANTINE BOOKS • NEW YORK

Library of Congress Catalog Card Number: 74-6234

SBN 345-24626-8-150

This edition published by arrangement with
William Morrow & Company, Inc.

First Printing: November, 1975

Printed in the United States of America

BALLANTINE BOOKS
A Division of Random House, Inc.
201 East 50th Street, New York, N.Y. 10022
Simultaneously published by
Ballantine Books, Ltd., Toronto, Canada

To Jean-Pierre Rudin, friend of books,
I give this book, and my friendship.

Part 1

Jeanne & Roland—
The Early Days

At eleven o'clock on the morning of January 17, 1955, Pandit Nehru, Prime Minister of India, held a Cabinet meeting to discuss how to deal with the famine devastating the plains of Bihar in the north of India. There had been no rain for three years, and the land was parched and cracked. The people and animals were shriveled to skeletons. Many finally died.

There were no easy solutions. Irrigate the Bihar with the waters of the Ganges, but that would take half a century to accomplish. Distribute food, but there was none to spare. Pray to the gods for rain, but they had been doing that since the beginning of time.

At eleven-thirty, a telephone call came from Bombay for the Prime Minister. His private secretary answered and explained that it was impossible to interrupt the Cabinet meeting. The man at the other end of the line, whom the secretary knew well, replied that *nothing was more serious or more important* than the subject that he must talk over with Nehru. The telephone was placed on the conference table. This was the "hot line," used only in case of fire in the Government Palace, disaster or war. The ministers waited uneasily as Nehru answered the call. The caller, whom he had known since childhood, urged him to drop everything else and come without delay to Bombay to discuss in secrecy a subject of momentous importance.

Nehru hung up the receiver and remained silent for several minutes. As always, a red rose bloomed in the third buttonhole of his white tunic. While he was staring off into space, a small, thin, polite smile played on his lips.

He finally looked at the men sitting around the table and excused himself, saying that for personal reasons he was forced to go to Bombay immediately. He asked them to solve the critical Bihar famine without him. After his departure, the ministers continued to discuss the Bihar problem, which remained as insoluble as before. Nehru's presence would not have affected the outcome.

The Prime Minister's private plane flew toward Bombay. He had left without hesitation because he loved and respected the old man who had called. Both a scholar and a saint, the old man had reached such a degree of inner purification that it was impossible for him to pronounce a false or unnecessary word.

As in governments the world over, the telephones of the Indian Government were tapped. Three foreign secret services already knew that Nehru was en route to Bombay to receive information "on which the future of the world would depend." Even before the plane had taken off from New Delhi, coded messages were being sent in all directions to warn governments, to inform colleagues in Bombay, to gather data about the caller, to procure all documents, photographs and information concerning the forthcoming conversation.

These messages were intercepted and decoded by other agents, and by the end of the day the various secret services were aware of the affair. Thus began an espionage battle that was to last for years and create an enormous number of victims in the ranks of the world's intelligence organizations. Yet, though they often had proof of the extreme importance of what they were looking for, at no time during their long search did any of the agents of any of the countries involved discover what it was really all about.

The plane landed in Bombay where, despite the winter season, the air was hot and sticky. As Nehru descended, his red rose started to wilt. It was the middle of the afternoon.

In Paris that night it was bitter cold. Jeanne Corbet had telephoned her husband that she would not be coming home that night. He understood. She never concealed anything from him.

She was twenty years younger than he. They had met when she took his course in cardiac pathology at the medical school. They had married, their first few years together had been serenely happy, and they had been quietly content ever since.

Intelligent, beautiful and ambitious, she would certainly have succeeded on her own. But her husband, a wealthy and eminent professor and doctor, had opened doors for her and spared her the usual delays. She became his assistant. They had an eleven-year-old son, Nicolas.

Jeanne had received satisfaction and even pleasure from her husband, and in return, she had given him tenderness, admiration, even desire. In short, they maintained a careful equilibrium and intelligent understanding in their private life, which included mutually enjoyable moments together in bed. For the past year, she had been having an affair. Her lover, Roland, had awakened in her such a fresh and intense passion that she was transformed. She had never before wanted another human being absolutely, which is to say that she had never really wanted another human being at all.

The consequences of the meeting in Bombay were to shatter their life and trample in the dust any plans they may have had for the future.

Chapter 1

An unescorted private car awaited Nehru at the Bombay airport. It took him to a beautiful, palatial house on the outskirts of the city. Servants opened the entrance gates and locked them behind him. The car drove up a path surrounded by immense trees and flower beds. The air smelled of damp soil, mangoes and sandalwood. After passing purple rhododendron bushes as high as chestnut trees, the car stopped at a small, modern one-floor building of ocher-colored brick. Nehru had often come there with his father, and then after his father's death, to talk with the venerable scientist whose wisdom was so precious to him.

He got out of the car, which was to wait for him. Much later, by cross-examining the chauffeur of the car, Jeanne Corbet was able to learn that Nehru had remained inside the building for over five hours.

When he arrived at the door, Nehru was astonished that he was not met by his host, who previously had always come to greet him on the doorstep. The door was open, and the corridors were empty. He entered the main hall, where ventilators were silently revolving on the ceiling. The walls were of white ceramic, broken up by bay windows through which he could see totally deserted laboratories that in the past had always been occupied by the scientist's assistants.

Halfway along the hall, two niches held two ancient, gilded bronze statues, one of Vishnu the Preserver of the World and the other of Siva the Triple-eyed Destroyer. Several faded petals and burnt-out sticks of incense lay

6

at their feet. Nehru took off his rose and placed it at the feet of Vishnu.

He finally arrived at the end of the corridor, where the main laboratory was located. Through the window, he saw two men dressed in white gazing intently at a small glass box in which a brown butterfly with blue markings was fluttering. One of the men saw him and drew his companion's attention to Nehru's presence. The second man, with a brown leathery face and impressive white beard, turned toward Nehru and smiled. His nose was large, his enormous eyes limpid and pure. Looking into those eyes gave one the feeling of peace, that good did exist in the world. He was a man of quiet strength and rare dignity.

Shri Bahanba was seventy-three. He belonged to a centuries-old, rich Brahmin family. During his studies in England, when India was still a colony, he had become passionately interested in all the physical sciences. On his return to India, he devoted himself to research and experiments on the basic life factor, the cell. His name and work were known to scientists the world over. Although he did not have a medical degree, he had made discoveries used by doctors and others working in the medical field, as Pasteur had done a century earlier. The marvels and horrors that he discovered each day under his microscope had confirmed his religious beliefs and encouraged him to continue on his road to spiritual purification.

Nehru clasped his hands before his face and bowed. The other two men did the same. Nehru moved to join them in the laboratory, but the door was locked. The younger of the two men, who appeared worried and tired, motioned to him to enter the adjoining laboratory. There, installed among tables covered with test tubes and other research material, he found an armchair facing the glass partition that separated the two rooms. On a small table next to the chair was a telephone. On the other side of the partition, the white-bearded man sat down on a lab stool facing Nehru. He picked up the telephone and motioned to Nehru to do the same; then the old man began to speak in English.

"Thank you for coming. And for having come so quickly. I do not think that we are being overheard. This telephone is not connected with the central telephone system, and my servants are watching the grounds so as to keep out intruders. I have taken all the essential precautions, but will take still another by abandoning English as everyone understands it."

He began to speak Sanskrit. Even in India, very few people know how to read this ancient sacred language, and those who know how to speak and understand it are even fewer in number. In order to express certain modern ideas, Bahanba was forced to make use of circumlocutions from time to time, but Nehru understood perfectly what the old man had to say to him. When Nehru came out five hours later, he stopped in the middle of the corridor between the two statutes of the gods, bowed with his hands joined together before each in turn, picked up the now completely withered rose that he had placed at the feet of the Preserver and lay it with deference before the Destroyer.

The man to whom the British Secret Service had assigned the affair knew Sanskrit, but he had been intercepted by the servants as he had tried to enter the grounds and had been conducted outside the gates. No one overheard what was said that day in the private grounds of Shri Bahanba. The inhabitants of what was known as Islet 307 learned about it later, and Jeanne Corbet learned about it from them.

Chapter 2

Jeanne awoke in the middle of the night and, by the dim light of a small lamp at the far side of the room, gazed at Roland as he slept peacefully by her side. His right hand still clasped the sheet to his stomach, so as to conceal from Jeanne his penis, which he found ridiculous in repose. She daydreamed about the several days they had been able to spend together in Morocco. They had rarely left the hotel and usually got out of bed only to swim, bask in the sun or eat on the terrace. They had eyes only for each other. The world around them served merely as a barely discernible background, a comfortable and exotic haze, a fragrant blur into which they nestled, protectively veiling their love. They had returned home tanned, rested, delighted. Jeanne leaned toward Roland's broad, smooth, muscular chest and caressed it with her lips. She felt an irresistible desire to lie down on top of him, to touch him everywhere with her body, aching with a painful, delightful sensation of desire. But he was sleeping so profoundly that she couldn't bear to disturb him.

She was thirsty and restless. The hideous plum-colored velvet curtains were drawn closed. She was beginning to love them, as she did the rest of this preposterous Left Bank apartment on the rue de Vaugirard that Roland had rented for their rendezvous. The bedroom and living room were crowded with curios, statuettes, furniture and lamps dating from Napoleon the Third and on up to the 1930s. Jeanne rose and went to the enormous kitchen, which was tiled in red and contained two gigantic stoves and enough cooking equipment to feed a regiment. The kitchen window looked out on the rear courtyard, and the transparent curtains were open. A young priest suffering from insomnia was gazing out of his window and saw Jeanne—naked, magnificent, abandoned—stride to and fro in the red kitchen and drink with voluptuous pleasure from a bottle of ice water. The garish light from the ceiling shone down on her face and arms and on the smooth reddish-brown hair that flowed to her shoulders. The red tiles on the floor gave a rosy reflection to the thighs of her long, graceful legs, to the small mahogany-colored triangle at the bottom of her belly, to her high, round, pointed breasts. When she turned out the light, the young priest knelt down to thank God for his blessings.

Jeanne returned to bed. Roland had not budged. She gently drew away the sheet and contemplated his nude body, so handsome and vulnerable that tears of happiness came to her eyes. She had not become accustomed, and would never be, to the miraculous joy it gave her to love him so intensely. She looked at his penis, in sleep as small as that of a child, and began to laugh quietly, with tender gratitude for the pleasures it had given her. Then she began gently to caress his belly, moving her hand downward till it reached his sex. It swelled under her touch, and Roland awakened.

Chapter 3

Immediately upon his return to New Delhi, Nehru arranged for meetings with heads of state of the world's major nations. He went first to the United States and had two separate conversations with President Eisenhower, then to Russia where he was received by Khrushchev, to China where he met with Mao, to Europe where he saw Chancellor Adenauer in Germany, Her Majesty Elizabeth II in Great Britain and President Coty in France. He also made a secret visit to General de Gaulle at his private home at Colombey. His travels were reported in the newspapers, and television cameras showed him smiling and shaking hands with all these political leaders. The journalists nicknamed him "The man with the rose" because of the flower that he always wore. Everyone thought the aim of his visits was to help ease the tensions of the cold war. He did everything possible to further this illusion, and perhaps he did have this in mind too. But the real objective of these meetings was far more important, so important that he obtained from men as dissimilar and opposed to each other as Mao, Eisenhower and Khrushchev immediate approval of the plan that he submitted to them.

Shri Bahanba's proposals could be effective only if they were carried out in absolute, inviolable secrecy. Nehru was assured of this. Each of his interlocutors understood what the consequences of the least indiscretion would be. Each of them also understood that the Bahanba plan required the unreserved collaboration of all the men whom Nehru had visited.

Success depended above all on the speedy execution of the necessary measures, which, indeed, they began to apply immediately after Nehru's departure from each capital. Less than a week after his visit with Eisenhower, the White House released a communiqué announcing that, due to the perhaps unjustified fears expressed by the Japanese and Canadian governments, the U.S. Department of Defense had decided to cancel the detonation of a high-powered underground nuclear bomb. The experiment had been scheduled to take place the following month on one of the Aleutian islands.

This decision was an essential part of the Bahanba plan and made its execution possible. The plan, however, had nothing to do with the cold war, a hot war or atomic experiments.

Two of the American rockets aimed permanently toward Russia were assigned a new objective. After Nehru's visit to Moscow, two Russian rockets were pointed in the same direction, and several years later, they were joined by the first of the long-distance Chinese rockets to be put into operation.

It was after Nehru's visits, as early as 1955, that a direct link was installed between Moscow and Washington, which was only revealed during the Administration of John Kennedy and baptized the "hot line." An identical hookup, but which remained secret, was established between Moscow, Peking and Washington.

These powerful nations lived in mutual fear and distrust, and their leaders were usually ready at the slightest provocation to utilize their war-making powers and bring the world closer to hell. But what Nehru had come to say to them was of such grave importance, and evoked such a high level of fear and hope, that the usual nationalistic and ideological antagonisms had to be set aside.

The secret services that had been aware of the affair since the Bombay interview received the order to report directly to their heads of state. These organizations were frequently involved in piecemeal operations the meaning of which was not revealed to them. Depending on the orders received, they fought each other or worked in collaboration, without ever knowing the whys and wherefores of what was going on. Those agents who came too close to the truth were liquidated. In the United States, the Mafia itself was used as a tool several times, and some of its members were sent to Europe as commandos. However, they believed they were working solely for Cosa Nostra.

Visits between heads of state cannot be improvised as quickly as those between friends and relatives. Although Nehru turned all the rules of protocol upside down, he was able to complete his visits only by November, 1955. When he finally returned to New Delhi, he was an apprehensive and haunted man, and he remained so until his death.

On each of his trips, he was accompanied by a second plane that landed after him and left again with him. No one ever saw any passenger alight from it. But, in each country, one or more visitors boarded the plane and descended hours later, looking frightened and anxious, the image of a brown butterfly with blue markings graven on their minds.

Chapter 4

When Nehru landed at New Delhi, the second plane that had accompanied him everywhere landed at Bombay.

Nine days later, in the early morning, Nehru opened the weekly Cabinet meeting. On the agenda was the famine in Calcutta as well as the old problem of the Bihar. The telephone on the table rang again. Nehru knew what he was going to hear before he picked it up. He was told that a fire during the night had completely destroyed the house and laboratories of Shri Bahanba. The fire had certainly been set with criminal intent. It had broken out everywhere, and the firemen had not been able to stop the blaze because the principal water main servicing that section of the city had been dynamited during the hour preceding the fire.

Surprised in their sleep, Shri Bahanba, several of his relatives, his principal collaborators and friends had perished. The authorities had not yet been able to search for bodies because the ruins were still ablaze.

Nehru slowly put down the phone. He was distressed and wretched, but the plan had to be inexorably carried out. For some time he had known he would never again see his old friend.

Chapter 5

The spring of 1955 marked the second year of Jeanne's and Roland's love affair. It seemed to them that they had only just started to know each other. The world had begun on the day they met, and that day began again each time they were together. But Roland's wife, who would never agree to a divorce, and his three children, a boy and two girls, were serious obstacles. Despite these problems, Roland was certain that one day soon everything would work out and that he and Jeanne would finally be able to live together, their future becoming ever more happy and bright. He thought in terms of eternity and never imagined that death could put an end to this joyous perfection. As fresh and naïve as an adolescent, he loved Jeanne with all the tenderness of his heart and the strength of his powerful male body. He was thirty-two when they met, and she was thirty-five. He gratified her heart, astonished her intelligence and satiated her body with such pleasure that each time they made love, she believed nothing could ever be the same again.

Such happiness was miraculous, and she knew this. She also knew that living together might very well change it. When she spent two or three days without seeing Roland, there were moments during which she found it impossible to breathe. If the separation continued, she began to suffer like an addict deprived of his drug. But she knew that he was suffering too and that the pain of these separations was perhaps what kept their love so passionate and complete. They were never bored together, never had time to develop those mundane routines whose accumulated weight can asphyxiate and bring banality to the most exceptional love. Above all, she he did not want them ever to have regrets. He had told her in September, after a long vacation with his family, that he could not take it any longer, that he was going to leave his family to live with her, even without a divorce. If she had encouraged him, perhaps he would have done so. But she remained silent, and he never spoke of it again. She knew that he adored his children and that if she forced him to leave them, she would lose him in the victory.

Winter had been extremely cold and spring late in coming. But at the end of April, the weather was lovely. Jeanne and Roland planned a five-day holiday in Normandy to see the budding trees and the flowering bushes and to walk along the sea.

But the day before they were to leave, Roland's three-year-old daughter awoke with the flu and a high fever, and Roland could not bring himself to leave. So the lovely springtime was wasted. They were never to have another, but of this they were happily unaware.

Nehru at that time had just left Moscow. During the days that followed, a doctor who had survived Stalin's trial of the "men in white" was rearrested, this time by Khrushchev, along with his entire family as well as his closest collaborators. They were all sent by plane to Si-

beria. The plane landed at a military airfield to refill its
tanks, flew off toward the east and was last seen above
the Sea of Okhotsk.

Chapter 6

Roland was handsome, tall and slim with an ath-
lete's build, his hair dark and curly, his eyes a large liquid brown, his hands fine and capable. He had worked
hard at the university, where he was an enormous success with the girls. He never neglected his studies to play
the role of Don Juan, though he did have several affairs. The most amorous and determined of his lovers
became pregnant, and he married her. It was a senseless
marriage for both of them. She was a pretty brunette
with large dark eyes and an angelic air. But in fact, she
was possessive, small-minded, garrulous, rather a crab
and incapable of sharing his thoughts and preoccupa-
tions. He tried his best to talk with her at her level, to
achieve some kind of communication, but she made that
impossible when she began to actively dislike him for
being "different."

She was, nevertheless, a sensual, seductive woman,
and when they made love, she became charming and
happy, her body opening for him ecstatically. In those
rare moments, they seemed to recapture the pleasure of
their premarital days. He knew she could not help being
as she was, that it was his own fault for having married
her, and so, despite her drawbacks, he felt a certain
tenderness for her, sometimes sad, sometimes amused.
He also felt gratitude for the beautiful children she had

borne him and had remained faithful to her until he met Jeanne. Roland continued to make love to his wife whenever she wanted. He felt guilty and did not feel he had the right to refuse her the simple pleasure he could still give her. But his body had an absolute yearning for Jeanne only, so that even when it participated in the act of pleasure, he felt no real sense of involvement.

Jeanne asked him about this one day, and he told her the truth. She had to make a great effort to control the savage jealousy that overcame her, but her intelligence and her faith in his love helped her to hide these feelings and finally conquer them. Everything that did not involve Roland seemed to her unreal; they and their love were the only meaningful things. She had even become estranged from her son. She did not love him less, but he came after Roland. She knew that if she were forced to choose between the two, she would only feign hesitation and distress.

Within a few days of meeting Roland, she had been transformed. Glowing with health and happiness, she seemed younger and more beautiful than in her adolescence. Her continual smile was contagious. She worked with more efficiency and speed and, never having thought much about how she dressed, now spent her free time shopping for clothes to please her lover. When her husband asked what had happened, she told him.

From then on, he had never entered her room, but if he had, would she have had the courage to refuse him? And if she had not refused him, wouldn't she have experienced more pleasure with him than before? She was so fantastically happy in heart and body that perhaps she would have been able to share that ecstasy with him. But he never came to her. Whether he came was of no importance, just as Roland's relations with his wife did not affect their love. There were Roland and Jeanne, and the rest did not exist.

Chapter 7

On a Saturday in June, 1955, a forty-two-year-old English biologist, Professor Adam Ramsay, took the plane for Brussels, where he boarded a Polish aircraft that took him behind the Iron Curtain. The world press made much of this departure, and the British public was shocked by the "desertion." Military experts declared that Ramsay was a specialist in bacteriological warfare. The British Government truthfully denied this contention. It became known that three of his colleagues and their families had been placed in solitary confinement. Even his maid and chauffeur, along with the latter's wife, had been arrested. The scientist's own wife and children had left earlier for Yugoslavia, where they disappeared from view. It was thought that they had rejoined Ramsay, but neither he nor his family appeared in Moscow or any of the other communist capitals.

The British public was even more shocked when it learned that at the time of the arrests, Jeep, the little Scotch terrier who had always accompanied the scientist to his laboratory, had been shot by the police and his body thrown into an incinerator.

Later in June, an expedition of American scientists and doctors boarded a special plan to Japan. This group of specialists in unicellular microorganisms was headed by a Harvard professor, Dr. Galdos. The plane landed at Hawaii and left again at midnight. The sky was clear, the weather good. Half an hour after its departure, radio contact was lost. No trace was ever found of the plane or its occupants.

One morning in early July, a fleet of automobiles drove into the driveway of the Galdos house in Cambridge, Massachusetts. At least fifteen men entered the house and kidnapped Mrs. Galdos and her sons as well as the two servants. A passing student became suspicious of so many cars surrounding the house and alerted the police, who intercepted the "convoy" as it was leaving the area. A shootout occured. The police were outnumbered, and two of them were killed. One of the kidnappers' cars was hit by a bullet, and crashed against the wall of an office building. The police identified the dead driver as a small-time gangster wanted by the New York police and a member of the Mafia.

Nehru arrived in Paris on September 2. Indian flags unfurled gracefully in the breeze along the Champs-Elysées. A black Citroen arrived at Villejuif, the Cancer Research Center, to pick up Professor Hamblain, Roland's superior, because one of the officials accompanying Nehru wanted to see him. Surprised and curious, Hamblain went willingly. The car took him to Orly and stopped in front of an isolated plane at the end of the runway, guarded by a security police car. Hamblain was invited into the plane. At the foot of the gangway, a French policeman and an Indian verified his identification. He climbed down the gangway an hour later, astounded and upset. The next day, he held a meeting with his closest associates. He asked if any of them had been suffering recently from eye problems. The unanimously negative answer seemed to relieve him greatly. Without explaining the reason for his questioning, he added that he was tired and intended to take a month's extra vacation. His assistant, Roland Fournier, would direct the work in his absence. He left immediately without shaking anyone's hand. He appeared both worried and elated.

Roland was surprised. Only the day before, Hamblain had told him that he had never felt better in his life, although for several days he had been having some trouble with his eyes. If this ailment continued, he intended to see his friend Dr. Ferrier for an eye examination.

At that time, Hamblain was fifty-two years old and a bachelor. He had no mistress as far as was known, and his colleagues jokingly maintained that he was still a virgin. He had a housekeeper who took excellent care of him. When he told her that they were going to depart immediately for Brittany, she protested that she couldn't leave without warning, that she did not like Brittany or the sea and that she would surely catch cold. He answered that he needed her help at his parents' home where he was going to visit, she would not catch cold and the healthy Breton air would be good for her. He forced her to come with him, but she did have time to pack her bag and complain to the baker and the grocer.

Roland telephoned Jeanne to tell her the bad news. They would have little time to see each other since this workload would be doubled due to his superior's absence. He added that their situation was becoming truly intolerable. Jeanne calmed him down, and they made a date for Sunday. He decided to tell his wife that he had work to do at the laboratory.

In the afternoon. Nehru had a long meeting with President Coty, then returned to the Indian Embassy. He came out at nine in the evening by way of a back door and got into his car, which took him to Colombey.

As soon as Nehru had left him, President Coty summoned the chief of the secret service department attached to the Presidency, Colonel P. He gave him detailed instructions that only succeeded in mystifying the Colonel, who requested explanations. The President answered that he couldn't give him any and commanded him to take first measures immediately. The Colonel objected that he didn't have enough personnel available to handle the second stage of the operation. The President replied that he would attend to that. When the Colonel had left, Coty asked General Koenig, Minister of National Defense, to come and see him at the Elysée as discreetly as possible. He asked him to recall from Algeria and place at his disposition within the next forty-eight hours a squad of parachutists. These men would never return to Algeria, would never again see their families. Little by little, one after the other, they would be listed as missing in action or killed in combat.

Dumfounded, the General protested, refused, demanded explanations. He reminded the President that he was a true republican and did not want to play any part in overthrowing the legal government. What did all this mean? What was going to happen to these parachutists? What were they going to do?

Solemnly, the President told him that it concerned something even more important than the preservation of France or the Republic. He could not tell him anything more than that, but according to the Constitution, he was Commander-in-Chief of the Army, and as such he demanded of the General obedience and silence. He added very softly, "Do I look like a man who wants to overthrow the Government?"

General Koenig stared at the kindly, mild, good-natured man and realized that the hypothesis was ridiculous. He agreed to do what was necessary.

Three days later, a military plane coming from Algiers landed at Le Bourget Airport outside Paris. Eight parachutists and a lieutenant disembarked. They were dressed in civilian clothes. Several of Colonel P.'s men took them by bus to a villa in the suburbs that had been requisitioned by the government. They stayed there awaiting further orders.

All telephone calls in and out of Pavilion L at the Cancer Research Center, where Roland and the staff of Professor Hamblain worked, were monitored. A truck belonging to the Gas Company of France arrived one morning at seven o'clock with a crew of workers to "change the gas pipes." Before the arrival of the laboratory personnel, two of the "gas employees" had had the time to conceal microphones in all the rooms. The others worked in the basement without bothering anyone. They left with the truck before the end of the afternoon.

The activity displayed for a week now by the Presidency's secret service had not escaped the attention of other French services or that of the foreign secret services. Pavilion L became the center of an incredible nest of spies and counterspies, none of whom knew what he was looking for, though each was convinced that all the others did know. Roland would have been surprised and bewildered if had been aware of what was going on. He was in a better position than anyone else to know that there was nothing secret about the work done at the pavilion. It was routine research, with constantly repeated examinations and experiments performed on laboratory animals. And if by luck something new was discovered, far from hiding it, the scientist immediately informed all those working in the same field.

Nevertheless, night and day, men were monitoring what was being said in Pavilion L, in the homes of Roland Fournier and other members of the staff, in the homes of the laboratory's two cleaning women and even in the apartment on the rue de Vaugirard where Roland and Jeanne had created their amorous paradise. The monitoring machines contained in their "brains" several key words that would trigger the warning signal no matter who said them, even though whoever pronounced these words would have no idea of their importance.

Here is where Samuel Frend became involved. He was a "cultural attaché" on the staff of the American Embassy in Paris. In reality, he was a military intelligence agent who took his orders directly from the Pentagon. He came to France with the Liberation Army, and had remained in Paris. Though profoundly American in his feelings, he had become very French in manner and thought. He had brought his wife and two children, a girl and a boy, from the States, and since that time two other sons had been born in Paris. He was thirty-nine years old, small and thin, with a lean, smiling face and a head fast becoming bald. His rather large ears stuck out a bit too much, and his little black eyes sparkled with gaiety and kindliness. He bought his clothes cheaply in the large department stores, and they always seemed slightly tight for him. He looked like a very nice man, which he was, and rather stupid, which he was not. He had made many friends in France and had his feelers out everywhere. Of course, the French police were aware of the real nature of his activities, but they did not attach much importance to them. Frend was, in fact, not a high-level agent but an ordinary functionary of American Intelligence. From time to time, he obtained good results because he was amiable, intelligent and above all insatiably curious, And, when necessary, he could be very enterprising indeed.

Within half an hour of the meeting between General Koenig and President Coty, Frend had been informed of it, and he was at Bourget to see the parachutists descend from the plane. He was the only one of all the agents keeping an eye on Pavilion L who knew that the mystery hidden there was preoccupying the President of France. Even Colonel P.'s subordinates themselves were not aware of this. However, Professor Hamblain's visit to Orly had escaped the attention of Frend, and he was not aware of the existence of Shri Bahanba. He believed the affair of Pavilion L to be purely French. It aroused his curiosity because of Presidential and military involvement. He had the villa in the suburbs watched to see what the parachutists were up to, and contacted his informers and brother agents swarming around the laboratory at Villejuif for information. He learned nothing. Nothing was happening. Obstinate as ever, he decided to talk to Professor Hamblain, who was vacationing in Brittany. He planned to disguise himself as a scientific journalist. One phrase, one word, might put him on the right track.

But at Quiberon he found the small house of the professor's parents empty. Their neighbor, a fisherman, who seemed to make a habit of watching tourists, gave him the information without hesitation. Frend had a talent for making people talk to him because he was a good listener. He learned that the previous morning the professor had been visited by English friends who had arrived aboard a small, rather old yacht named *The Cat's Smile,* and that everyone had left sometime in the afternoon of the same day.

"Everyone?" Frend said.

"The professor, his father and mother, and even the maid he had brought from Paris. I went down to the port with them. Old M. Hamblain was not very happy about leaving. He has rheumatism, and this is hardly the season for a cruise. He was a schoolteacher in the old days and is now retired. His wife always agrees with anything her son wants. But you should have heard the old Parisan maid! She said to her employer: 'You're crazy. I've never been on a boat. I'm going to be sick!' He just laughed and made fun of her. He looked happy, as though he were leaving on a honeymoon. Surely not with that old nut! What an idea, to take your maid on a cruise! She would have been better off staying here to take care of the house. It's none of my business, but still. . . ."

"Do you know where they were headed?"

"Portugal. Then the Mediterranean. It's normal in this season to look for the sun, although the weather has been pretty fine here."

On his return to Paris, Frend immediately sent a coded radio report to the Pentagon. He gave a description of *The Cat's Smile* and advised them to arrange an "ac-

cidental" meeting at sea. Perhaps a collision. A ship-
wreck would enable them to pick up Professor Hamblain, who certainly possessed the information about
something of vast importance that the English also knew
about. This detail made the officer who recieved the report leap to his feet. Of course, he knew nothing about
the Bahanba plan and the dominant role played in it by
the United States, since the Pentagon was only an un-
knowing participant.

The Cat's Smile was found by an American submarine six days later. A fire had completely destroyed the
yacht, with only the half-burnt-out shell remaining.
There was no trace of its passengers. The commander of
the American submairne radioed for instructions and
followed with his periscope the wreckage, which floated
toward the southwest.

Another American submarine was cruising in the
area, actually 7,500 miles from the place where it was
officially supposed to be. It picked up the message, decoded it and sent it to Washington. Three hours later,
the commander of the submarine that had found the
wreckage recieved the order to burn whatever might remain of *The Cat's Smile* before it sank, then to forget
the incident. Neither the discovery nor the destruction of
the yacht was to figure in the submarine's official or confidential log.

Roland had succeeded in freeing himself from work
and family for the afternoon and night of September 21,
1955. He rejoined Jeanne in a little Polynesian restaurant off the Champs-Elysées, completely unaware of
what had happened to his superior, whom he believed to
be happily fishing for shrimps, his nose red and his feet
icy cold from the Breton waters.

Chapter 8

Roland and Jeanne made a habit of trying out all the exotic foreign restaurants in Paris, to get a taste of the rest of the world. Neither of them had done much traveling. They enjoyed anticipating the pleasures in store for them when one day they could leave hand in hand to look at foreign lands. One day, but when? It just didn't occur to them that obstacles might arise to prevent them from traveling and making love whenever they pleased. Roland believed in this vague but radiant future with childish faith, never asking himself how it could come about. Jeanne dreamed of it without really believing in it.

They left the restaurant, the taste of the hot exotic sauces still burning their mouths and their hearts light and gay. Roland suggested that they climb to the top of the Arc de Triomphe. Like most Parisians, they had never done this before. They played at being tourists. He spoke to her in German, which she did not understand. She answered in Spanish, and he pretended not to understand. As they walked up the Champs Elysées, they stared into shop windows, commenting to each other on the various items displayed. Holding Jeanne by the hand, Roland, with an incomprehensible accent, asked a policeman the way to the Eiffel Tower. He then thanked him effusively and dragged Jeanne in the opposite direction. Jeanne burst out laughing. Behaving in such an idiotic fashion made her feel like a young girl.

The weather had been sunny, clear and warm since the beginning of July. Paris was dry as a biscuit. The leaves on the chestnut trees leading to the Place de la Concorde were beginning to shrivel. Near the Arc de Triomphe, the leaves of the plane trees were still hanging onto the branches, but they seemed to be made of dehydrated parchment ready to fall at any moment. The passersby strolled along, happy and tired, as though still on vacation. Clad in gay summer dresses, all the women looked young and pretty.

Jeanne was dressed in an ankle-length copper-colored skirt and a light silk sweater of apple green. Just for fun, she carried a little straw umbrella. Her seductive body looked fulfilled and triumphant as she strode beside Roland.

A strong west wind began to blow, so that the flags of a visiting African president flew wildly about on their poles and swirling clouds of dust rose from the sidewalks. Above the noise of the traffic, the sounds of a distant storm could be heard. Clouds were beginning to fill the sky.

When Roland and Jeanne reached the top of the Arc de Triomphe, mingling with the blissful tourists, a great gust of wind began to sweep toward the city, flooding the suburbs with rain. To the west, the straight lines of the avenues of the Grande-Armée and Neuilly were already darkening, and leaves wrenched from the trees by the wind were whirling up toward the clouds in the sky. To the east, the sky was full blue and the sidewalks of the Champs-Elysées dazzled the eye with the colors of the women's clothes. Suddenly, there was a stupendous burst of thunder and lightening, and torrents of rain inundated the summit of the arch. The toursits raced for shelter. Jeanne and Roland, their arms around each other, their eyes closed, stood alone under her yellow parasol, listening to the flood or rain pouring down on them and on the world.

An hour later, they were in each other's arms, nude in their bed on the rue de Vaugirard, with all the curtains drawn closed, a fire glowing in the room. They continued their exotic voyage by exploring the country, always the same and ever unknown, that each offered up to the other. Outside, there were repeated earsplitting claps of thunder, and the rain fell in torrents on the walls and roofs of the surrounding buildings. Oblivious to all of this fury, Jeanne and Roland knew only their world of ecstasy.

The ears of the person monitoring what went on in that room began to burn and his face turned scarlet.

Chapter 9

The next day, the lovers found it impossible to see each other, but Roland telephoned Jeanne twice. The day after that, at ten in the morning, he called to say he would meet her at five-thirty in the afternoon at the rue de Vaugirard apartment.

In the course of this conversation, he innocently pronounced the key word, which was heard by all the secret services listening in. It was such a banal phrase that it was picked up only by the two men working for Colonel P., one of whom knew that those words were a warning signal. They notified the Colonel, who immediately set into motion the special measures he had worked out following the general directives handed him by the President. Between three-thirty and four that afternoon, four ambulances entered the Research Center at Villejuif and left after a quarter of an hour.

One of Samuel Frend's men followed them as far as Le Bourget, but couldn't get any farther because the doors of the hangar they entered were closed tight behind them.

At four-thirty, an explosion rocked Pavilion L, and within seconds it was transformed into a single bizarre flame. The heat was so intense that all the metal melted completely. Despite the heroic efforts made by the firemen, the pavilion was still burning at midnight.

Alerted by the fire officer, the Colonel-in-Chief of the Paris firemen came to inspect the scene. He was astonished at the intensity of the heat and that the water, instead of diminishing the flames, seemed to increase them. He knew of no substance capable of burning this way, but he had heard of new incendiary bombs that the Army had stocked in its secret arsenal. Could that be possible? But then why? And why the pavilion? He could only do his duty and make a report.

The flames subsided a little before dawn. During the night, the sections of the walls still remaining upright glowed like enormous furnaces. The heat they radiated burned the face of anyone who came within fifty yards of them. None of the occupants of the pavilion had been able to escape. There was little hope of finding any remains.

Samuel Frend's man watched the hangar at Le Bourget all night, but in vain. The ambulances had left again by another door that was not in his line of vision.

While Pavilion L was burning, Frend followed the fifth ambulance into which had climbed the last three parachutists he had once followed to the secret villa. One of them drove and, after entering Paris, had crossed the Seine and taken the rue de Vaugirard.

Jeanne had undressed, bathed, perfumed herself. She had then put on the russet-velvet bathrobe that Roland liked. Whenever he opened it to look at her nude body, he told her she resembled a ripe apricot.

As she placed the tea on the low, fake Napoleon III Chinese lacquer table, she smiled, thinking that once again the tea would be cold before they would be ready to drink it.

He was late, but she waited patiently until six o'clock. Soon after that, she became worried and telephoned Pavilion L and obtained a busy signal. She kept phoning every few minutes but finally stopped calling, afraid that Roland might be trying to reach her and would find the line busy. At seven, she called six times in succession and always obtained the same busy signal. She dialed the operator but hung up before there was an answer because the doorbell rang. Roland never rang the bell, but perhaps he had forgotten his key. Jeanne ran to the door and opened it.

Two short, thickset men with army crew cuts and wearing white overalls pushed the door wide and entered. She thought they might be laboratory associates of Roland's, that something had happened to him and that he had sent them to take her to him. Before she had time to think further, one of the two men stepped behind her and threw her robe up over her shoulders, imprisoning her arms, while the other covered her face with a pad of cotton wool doused in an anesthetic.

She recognized the odor of the anesthesia immediately and knew it to be so effective and violent that her husband had always hesitated to use it on his patients. She turned her head quickly, twisted away from her attackers and began to scream. The man facing her, dazzled by her nudity and confused by her cries, dropped the cotton gag and began to struggle with her. She bit his cheek savagely, and he yelled out. Beneath the window, in the second courtyard, an ambulance siren and then police sirens began to shriek.

"Good god. The cops. We have to take her. Idiot. What did you do with the cotton?"

As the man Jeanne had bitten bent to pick up the anesthetic, Jeanne struck him in the face with her knee, smashing his nose. Swearing, he straightened up and was about to receive a terrible karate blow but parried it just in time. The orders were to avoid violence at all cost.

He tried to take her by the knees and lift her in the air, but she kicked him in the neck, knocking him down. She freed herself of her second attacker by tearing off her bathrobe, then ran to the other end of the room, opened the window and screamed for help. The ambulance drove around the large courtyard at full speed, followed by a police car. Another car blocked the entrance to the outer courtyard. There was such a great deal of shouting that no one paid any attention to Jeanne's screams except the two men who had assaulted her. They fled down the staircase and fell into the arms of the police. They defended themselves savagely, but they weren't armed. Their mission seemed completely stupid and incomprehensible to them.

Colonel P., his headphones clamped over his ears, had followed the entire operation. Enraged, he asked himself who had alerted the police. Now he was going to be forced to have those three imbeciles released, hush up the scandal, suppress the reports, lose precious time. And then start in all over again. That damned female was still in circulation! He thought it over. After all, she had not been the one to pronounce the key word. It would be enough to continue to listen in on her conversations. There were even microphones hidden in her home. Perhaps she would never say the words. Perhaps it would have been better not to have meddled with her just yet. Luckily, everything had gone well at Villejuif.

Among the curious massed in front of the entrance, there was a small man who innocently looked on. Slipping behind the policemen and into the inner courtyard, he walked right by the officers fighting with the two men in white, climbed the stairs, entered the apartment, found Jeanne putting on her dress, showed her a tricolored official-looking card and introduced himself. "Superintendent Frend. You've had a narrow escape." He answered her questions evasively, threw a coat over her shoulders and requested her to accompany him. Passing the police who were now rushing up the stairs, he gestured with his hand over his shoulder, saying to them, "Up there." Then, he pushed Jeanne gently toward the street, put her into his black car parked several yards away and immediately drove off.

It was Frend who had alerted the police when he saw the ambulance drive down the rue de Vaugirard. Using the radio transmitter in his car, he had spoken on the Paris police headquarters wavelength and given orders directly to the police cars. He hoped that the clash between the policemen and the parachutists would create a certain amount of confusion that would enable him to pick up some information.

Just as he was leaving the apartment, Frend had put in his pocket the wad of cotton soaked in anesthetic. At the red light at the corner of the rue de Vaugirard and the rue de Rennes, he shoved it over Jeanne's face as she opened her mouth to ask him a question. Choking with surprise, she breathed in quite a bit of the vapor before breaking loose. Since he did not want to have to carry her, he did not persist and threw the cotton out of the car window. Half-conscious, she fought against sleep and the mist closing in on her. He stopped the car in the courtyard of a private building on the rue Boissy d'Anglas, where they entered an apartment on the ground floor, followed a long corridor, went down a staircase, took an elevator and finally ended up in Frend's small office within the American Embassy. When Jeanne was quietly sitting in a chair, he wiped the sweat off his forehead and sighed. He had taken enormous risks. He had never before ventured to take such initiatives on his own. He hoped that the affair was as important as he suspected. Otherwise. . . .

He went out into the hall and came back with two paper cups full to the brim with hot coffee. This woman knew something, and she must tell him what she knew. There was no question of sleeping. . . .

Chapter 10

"All right," Frend said. "I don't know anything about all this. I'm asking you to explain it to me."

Jeanne knew nothing. She shook her head, still half-drugged and bewildered by the incomprehensible events. But her heart was full of anguish. Roland. What had happened to Roland?

Forty-five minutes later, sitting inside the black car, she was staring at the hellish flames of the Pavilion L fire, at the firemen, the police, the onlookers moving about like obscure silhouettes against a changing kaleidoscope of light.

She stared at the fire, and Frend stared at her. He pointed to the flames and said, "He's in there," hoping that in her despair she would let the truth pour out. She only sobbed like a child.

He asked in a low voice, "Why?"

She slowly shook her head. She didn't know anything. Finally, he was convinced she was telling the truth. However, Jeanne was still in danger, so he offered to take her back to the Embassy, where she would be safe. Again she shook her head. Her safety wasn't important. Her world had become fire and darkness, grief and death. She closed her eyes and didn't move.

Frend backed out of the courtyard and drove Jeanne to the rue de Varennes, where she and Professor Corbet lived in a private house that opened onto lovely gardens. Leading her as though she were blind, Frend placed her in the hands of her husband.

"She'll tell you who I am and what happened. There

33

was an attempt to kidnap her. She's half-drugged and in
a deep state of shock. I think it would do her good to
sleep it off. I'm sure she'll talk to you tomorrow. Keep
an eye on her and don't leave anything dangerous within
her reach."

He was silent for a few seconds, then added, so that
his warning would be taken seriously, "Fournier is
dead."

Paul Corbet wasn't surprised that a stranger seemed
to be aware of Roland Fournier's love affair with his
wife. He thought only of what she must be going
through.

He put her to bed, gave her a sedative and called in a
nurse to stay beside her. Little Nicolas was already
asleep and therefore spared the shock of seeing how
ghastly his mother's face had become.

Frend spent the rest of the night receiving reports
from his agents and writing his own. He went home to
kiss his children before they left for school and eat his
Parisian breakfast of coffee with milk and croissants.

Frend's wife, Susan, no taller than he, was plump and
good-humored. Frend was extremely fond of her and
grateful to her for causing him so few complications in
his personal life, his professional life being so extremely
complicated. Their eldest son, Colin, kissed them both
good-bye before leaving for his courses in science at the
Sorbonne. At seventeen, he was tall and skinny, and
with his blond hair and slouching walk resembled a
cornstalk swaying in the wind. His parents constantly
wondered aloud how they had come to produce such a
slim giant who didn't seem to resemble either of them.

The best way to communicate with someone whose
telephone is tapped and whose mail is inspected is to
send them a letter by special messenger. A little after
three in the afternoon, Paul Corbet, who had canceled
all his appointments and his university classes for the

day, received such a letter addressed to his wife. She
was still asleep, so he opened the letter. It was a message
from Samuel Frend. As soon as Jeanne woke up, he
showed it to her. In an instant, she had recovered her
will to live. The message said: "Roland Fournier is not
dead. I can give you proof of this. The fire was only a
camouflage. I don't know where Fournier is, but if you
will help me, together we will find him."

The letter also revealed that the Corbet home on the
rue de Varennes was full of hidden microphones and that
the three telephones were monitored night and day. He
advised her not to discuss important or private affairs
with her husband except in their car or in the garden.
He made a date with her for the next day at three
o'clock in the afternoon, promising to send a car for her.

The rain fell in torrents. Jeanne and her husband put
on raincoats and, sheltered under a large umbrella,
walked up and down the garden paths, which were covered with autumn leaves. They inhaled the odor of wet
ground, humid air, soaked bark. Paul Corbet listened to
his wife's incredible story of what had happened. From
time to time, he asked a question to clarify details.
When he recalled that moment in the years that followed, the odors and the sound of the rain falling
seemed so real to him that he had the impression that he
was wet through and through once again.

He was surprised that the police hadn't come to interrogate his wife. He had read only a few lines in the
morning newspaper *Le Figaro* about the fire at Villejuif,
and they did not give any indication of its importance.

From the first moment, he had made up his mind to
help Jeanne. As soon as they had reentered the house,
without paying any attention to the telephone taps, he
called the central police station of the Sixth Ward, introduced himself, declared that his wife had been subjected
to an attempted kidnapping the evening before and
asked how the investigation was coming along.

At first, there was silence at the other end, then whispers in the distance. The call was transferred, then a courteous voice informed him that there had been no investigation because there had not been an attempted kidnapping. The false hospital attendants had been in fact real attendants who had come to pick up a mentally disturbed patient and had simply made a mistake in the address.

The policeman rang off, but Paul Corbet hung on and said, "Damn all you bastards listening in. I'm going to get to the bottom of this. And don't think that fear of a scandal can scare me out of it."

Dr. Corbet was a well-built man who seemed ten years younger than his age. Tall, broad-shouldered, with gray hair clipped short, he looked more like a retired football player than a rich and famous professor and doctor. At first lacking influential friends or patrons, he had nevertheless become one of the five greatest cardiac specialists in the world.

He realized that he wouldn't get at the true reasons for such a senseless series of events without going directly to the upper echelons of government. He called the office of the Prime Minister, Edgar Faure, who, though strong as an oak tree, came to see him at the beginning of each year for a heart checkup.

Faure's private secretary replied that the Prime Minister was too busy to answer the call, but Corbet shouted and insisted. Disconcerted, and fearing God knows what the doctor might have discovered wrong with Faure's heart, the secretary put him through.

As a matter of fact, Edgar Faure *was* busy and surprised at the urgency of the call. But he became fascinated by the story Corbet told him. Faure promised he would do everything possible to clear up the mystery and would call Corbet back the following day.

The Prime Minister had barely hung up when his telephone rang again. It was President Coty, informing him that he would like to see him.

An official messenger on a motorcycle delivered a hand-written message to Corbet from President Coty early that evening. Corbet was to come to the Elysée Place that same evening at nine. The President apologized for any inconvenience this impromptu invitation might cause, but indicated that the matter was important.

Until that moment, Corbet had only half-believed Frend's assertions of the responsibility of the Presidency's secret service in the events of the pervious day. It had sounded too much like a fantasy. He hadn't even mentioned it to Edgar Faure. But this invitation shook his doubts. Or, could it be that the President was worried about his heart? He didn't think so, but, just in case, he took along his medical bag.

Before leaving, he made sure that Jeanne was securely locked in her room and left his revolver with her.

Jeanne waited calmly for his return. After the agony of believing Roland dead, she felt tranquil and was sure that it would simply be a question of finding him. In the quiet, she listened to the beating of her heart and to the rain falling in the garden.

Her mind kept returning to Roland. How could she have believed he was dead? That was absurd. Roland could not die because their love could not die. All she could think was, we will be together again.

Paul Corbet returned home after an hour. Disconcerted, he told her what had transpired with the President at the Elysée Palace.

"Coty didn't explain anything. He asked me to stop my investigation and not to do anything that might cause a scandal. He assured me that no one wanted to hurt you. He made me swear not to reveal what he was going to tell me, then he told me nothing! All he would say was that the welfare of the entire world depended on the resolution of this problem."

"But what on earth does this have to do with me?"

"That's what I asked the President. He looked completely dismayed and said, 'I can't tell you anything. Don't ask me anything more. Don't do anything. Don't talk about this to anybody. I can promise you that Madame Corbet won't be bothered again.' "

"But Roland. Did you ask him where Roland is?"

"The same answer. 'I can't tell you anything, I don't know anything.' I had the impression that he thought he already knew too much and that he would give up the Presidency not to know it. He asked me to promise not to try to get to the bottom of all this. He was obviously extremely upset."

"Did you promise him?"

"Yes. If it's an official affair of state or, worse yet, an affair of states in the plural, it's better not to get involved."

While he was answering Jeanne's questions, he pointed at the ceiling, the walls and his ears, to make her understand he was speaking in this fashion because they were probably being bugged. She nodded to show she understood.

"Besides, my promise depended on the President's assurance you would never be victimized again. I'm saying this so that anyone listening can hear. If you are left alone, I'll remain quiet. Otherwise. . . . Do you know what he said as I was leaving? He shook my hand warmly and thanked me for being so understanding, and then he added: 'If unavoidable circumstances should occur, if it becomes necessary to bother Madame Corbet again, I beg you to tell her not to resist, but to give in immediately.' "

Chapter 11

The following morning, sitting in the garden where the sun shone down on the scattered leaves still wet from the night rains, Paul Corbet talked with his wife about the possible ways of dealing with the situation. He had given his word but only for himself, and Jeanne was not committed to inaction because of his promise. He would arrange for her to have all the assistance he could provide. She thanked him, not at all surprised by his attitude. A thousand times he had given her proof that his love for her had only one aim—to make her happy whatever the cost or reason.

"The meeting this afternoon might be a trap," Paul said. "We have no proof that it was actually Frend who sent the note. You aren't familiar with his handwriting. The car that is to come to pick you up might be simply an attempt to succeed in the kidnapping that failed. I'll accompany you."

But the car didn't come.

Jeanne felt the hope that had sustained her for the last twenty-four hours diminish by the minute. She was persuaded that Roland was still alive, but Frend had promised *proof*.

She waited for two hours, then could no longer contain herself. She phoned for a taxie to take her to the United States Embassy, where she was informed that nobody named Samuel Frend was on their staff. However, she knew Ambassador Douglas Dillion well, as they had often met at various Parisian social functions. She asked to see him. He received her warmly and asked to what he owed such a charming visit. Jeanne realized that he knew nothing about what had happened. She told him she had come to see a friend, Samuel Frend, and that she had been informed he didn't exist! Dillion looked astonished and made a telephone call. When he was through on the phone, he sat shaking his head and said:

"My dear friend, there is such a person as Samuel Frend, but he no longer works here. That is, he has been recalled to Washington. He left last night. No, he won't be back. At least I don't think so, since he took his family with him. His career in Europe is over."

The next day, Jeanne left for Washington.

Chapter 12

Thus began Jeanne's incredible search for Roland, a quest that would take seventeen years. Other women have been known to wait a lifetime for the return of an adventurous lover or a vanished husband, but Jeanne was not a woman to merely await the denouement of events. She traveled the world over and faced danger countless times. She found traces of Roland's trail, then lost them in the intricacies and intrigues of the various secret services she came up against. It seemed to her that the intelligence agencies were hiding some truth she must not discover and that they themselves did not really comprehend.

She fought with all her strength against the mystery, hoping by the very violence of her effort to tear away at the wall of secrecy. There were times when she was so exhausted that she returned home to her husband to regain strength. He always continued to help her with his money, intelligence and contacts. She was astonished at each return to find him looking older and her son more grownup. Nicolas had left childhood and become an adolescent in her absence. When she saw him, Jeanne read in his eyes love, fear, admiration and all the questions he dared not ask. He knew that she was going to all the countries of the world, fighting to discover a secret that did not even have a name. She was his heroine. He was very handsome, tall and slender, unlike his father, with the blue-eyed gaze of a forlorn Irishman. Occasionally, in Paris after yet another failure, she was tempted to abandon her search and to live in peace with her adoring son and her inexorably aging husband who had given her so much. But she could not forget Roland. Without him, she felt like a deep-sea diver who knows that the life-saving air is just above if he can only rise to the surface. She felt suspended in a void, waiting for the miracle that would bring her back to reality.

Jeanne was fascinated by the shrouded mystery that at times she came close enough almost to touch but that escaped her clutch just as she made to seize it. She was now convinced that the mystery must affect all of humanity, for only such a great secret would cause the most powerful nations to come together in its defense, for once putting aside their most violent disagreements.

She had been in London for two months when the new attempt to kidnap her took place. She had been trying to find a trace of the English "friends" who had picked up Professor Hamblain at Quiberon. The only thing she had been able to discover was that *The Cat's Smile* was a false name, since it was not inscribed on any insurance list. The ship's real name and the identifying markings had undoubtedly been falsified once it had left British waters.

After spending an hour in the offices of Lloyd's Insurance Company, she entered a taxi to return to the hotel.

Two men followed her into the taxi, which drove away at full speed. She was not afraid since she had forseen that something like this might happen and was prepared for it. She put her hand in her purse and shot her revolver through it, killing the two men. The driver was wounded in the shoulder and lost control of the taxi, which crashed against a parked bus.

In less than four hours, Scotland Yard had taken charge of the investigation from the police station in the area and then transferred the case to a special office of the Ministry of the Interior. The next morning, at her hotel, Jeanne was visited by a gray-haired man sporting a small reddish mustache, who asked her to come with him.

"Where?"

"I can't tell you."

"How can you think I would accept an invitation like this after what has just happened to me?"

"I can promise you that you'll be perfectly safe."

"You can promise whatever you want, but I have no reason to believe you."

"Of course, you're right. It's unfortunate. I guess I'd better go."

Just as he was leaving, she declared she would accompany him. She could not let an opportunity pass to learn something new. Since her revolver had been taken by the police, she took another from her suitcase and openly put it in her coat pocket. The man smiled politely.

A large black car awaited them and drove them to Buckingham Palace. Jeanne handed over her revolver to the man with the reddish mustache, and three minutes after her arrival, she was received by the Queen of England.

Elizabeth spoke to her with exquisite kindliness and courtesy "as one woman to another." She told her she understood perfectly her actions and her obstinacy. But she declared that Jeanne's investigation would lead to nothing and could even be harmful to mankind. And she, Elizabeth, was certain that Jeanne did not want to injure her fellowman.

No, of course she did not want to do that.

Then, would she give up her search? All women, even those whose position places them above all others, could suffer from pain due to love. When the public interest is at stake, one must learn to forget one's own anguish.

"I'm sorry," replied Jeanne." But I can't give up."

"I was afraid of that," the Queen said gravely. "But I had to ask you to do it. May I give you a piece of advice?"

"I would be greatly honored."

And Elizabeth II, the British Queen, used almost the identical words as René Coty, the French President, to recommend that if Jeanne were the victim of another kidnapping attempt, she should not defend herself.

En route alone from Buckingham Palace to her London lawyer's office in the black automobile, Jeanne thought over the Queen's advice. A curious image haunted her memory—the Queen's handbag, black and of excellent quality but not very chic, that Elizabeth had clasped tightly in her hand as though it had been she herself who was paying a visit. Jeanne put this absurd detail from her mind. She was to be confronted with the wounded taxi driver that same afternoon. She hoped he would answer the questions posed by the police inspectors. But when she arrived at her lawyer's office, he informed her that the wounded man had been kidnapped from the prison infirmary by two bogus policemen with papers that were seemingly in order. They had said they had come to take the man to the inspectors for the confrontation by Jeanne.

Jeanne then decided to follow the advice that had been given to her twice and not to put up any struggle if they came to take her, no matter what dangers might be involved. But she waited in vain, for there was no further kidnapping attempt.

Chapter 13

At the very beginning of her search for the truth about Roland's disappearance, when Jeanne had decided to leave for Washington to find Samuel Frend, she had had a taste of the difficulties to be surmounted at every turn.

It took her three months to pick up Frend's trail again, and when she did succeed in finding him—at the American Embassy in Montevideo, where he was a member of the staff—he denied ever having met her. He knew perfectly well that she was aware that he was lying, but he let it be understood that it was useless for her to insist.

For two weeks, she tried vainly to meet him again, until she learned that he was no longer working at the Embassy. The Paris scenario was repeated.

She returned to France and began an investigation there, aided by a private detective named Poliot, a retired police inspector, asthmatic, with a full face and a round belly. He rode around Paris on a bicycle as old as himself, wearing a derby hat that had served as his umbrella for twenty years. He had an invaluable knack for making concierges and tradesmen tell him everything he wished to know.

Poliot informed Jeanne that Roland Fournier's wife, mad with grief, had not been able to tolerate the thought of remaining in Paris. With her three children, she had left for Corsica to stay with her parents. Thanks to the concierge, Poliot had been able to enter the apartment. He had found it empty, cleaned and repainted by the new tenant, who had not yet moved in. Not one speck of dust had remained to provide any leads.

But he did bring back one curious piece of information: the truck carrying Madame Fournier's furniture and all her husband's books and papers to the port at Nice for transportation to Corsica had caught fire en route. It had burned like a handful of phosphorus, leaving only ashes and twisted metal.

A fire exactly like the one at Villejuif!

Jeanne ran up against fire for the third time when she went to Quiberon after having learned about the disappearance at sea of Roland's superior. The same neighbor who had given information to Samuel Frend showed her the blackened ruins of the house of Professor Hamblain's parents which had burned down entirely a week after the departure of *The Cat's Smile*. The lame fisherman shrugged his shoulders and said it had been a terrible catastrophe, fate if you will, with the family lost at sea and the house destroyed.

On her return to Paris, Jeanne received a new report from Poliot. Professor Hamblain's brother, his only remaining relative, had taken all the furnishings away from the apartment, including any papers that might have been there. Poliot had visited the place and had found it completely renovated, just as Fournier's had been, and apparently by the same people, who had used the same color paint and scraped and polished and cleaned it up with exactly the same care.

Since Professor Hamblain was not yet considered legally dead, the removal of his furniture and belongings and the revamping of the apartment was, to say the least, ususual, if not illegal. Poliot had taken it on himself to talk to the professor's brother. He was unable to find him, for the simple reason that the professor had no brother. The furniture and documents had disappeared, God knows where.

Chapter 14

During the first six months of her search, Jeanne's telephone was tapped and she was spied upon constantly. She caught on to this almost immediately. The men following her did not try to hide, but if she accosted them and attempted to ask questions, they slipped away from her and disappeared. When she crossed a frontier, the agents of the country she was leaving passed her on as in a relay race to those of the country she was entering. At the end of the sixth month, her followers disappeared. Her movements continued to be watched and reported, but there were no more eavesdroppers because those who had given the orders to listen in knew that by now she no longer could pronounce the key phrase.

The London kidnapping attempt took place only a year later. Therefore, it was for another reason entirely that they tried to seize her at that time. When, on arriving at the end of her search, Jeanne learned the truth, her regret for having resisted gave rise to an unmitigated, desperate, deadly remorse that froze her heart.

Chapter 15

Roland Fournier's wife and children, now living in the village of Santa Lucia de Moriano in Corsica, had also been under close surveillance. But this surveillance, like Jeanne's, also ceased after six months. Roland's wife believed that he was dead. Her violent despair soon ended. She was given an enormous pension that was much too high in relation to what her husband had earned when alive, but she accepted it as being perfectly normal. In June, 1957, she met a rich widower, a Corsican pharmacist of some fifty years, named Dominique Cateri. Having had some occasional business dealings with the Italian Mafia, he had been put in charge of a plan that involved Madame Fournier, though of this she was unaware.

On June 17, at the end of the afternoon, she went to the small studio that Cateri had rented near the beach for his vacation and made love with him for the first time. She was very happy, all the more so because she had been deprived of sexual pleasure ever since Roland's supposed death.

When she returned to pick up her children who had been left to play at the seaside, she was told that they had gone for a sail with "friends" in a superb red boat. Neither the boat nor the children were seen again.

Her capacity for grief soon exhausted, she married the pharmacist, who had fallen in love with her extraordinary sensuality. Jeanne saw her in Bastia in 1967, reigning over the cash register at the pharmacy. She had become a widow once again, had grown quite fat and

wore several large diamond rings along with her two
wedding bands. Her disposition had sweetened consider-
ably.

Chapter 16

Fire continued to figure in each phase of the
search. Jeanne met it for the fourth time thanks to
something her husband had read in an English medical
magazine, *The Lancet,* during his flight home from Teh-
eran, where he had been called on consultation. Three
pages of the magazine were devoted to the great Indian
scientist, Shri Bahanba, recalling the dramatic circumstances of his death years before in a Bombay fire. Paul
Corbet was struck by the resemblance of this fire to that
of Villejuif, as well as the similarity of Bahanba's work
to that of Hamblain and his group.

When Corbet arrived back in Paris, Jeanne had already left again, and he had to wait for her return to tell
her about the *Lancet* article. At that time, she was
trying to find a way to meet those Americans who were
engaged in or knowledgeable about the work being done
in bacterological warfare. Like everyone else, she knew
that all over the world military laboratories were preparing an apocalypse greater than even a total atomic war
could bring. She had searched in Paris, London, Munich, Milan, and Zurich for a connection with the events
at Villejuif, but to no avail. From a French secret agent
who had been to Warsaw, she had received information
about what was being produced in Soviet laboratories,
but their work was similar to that being done in Europe,
except perhaps for the quantity of their production. And

this difference was negligible since a quart of poison from one of the virulent organisms developed by the labs, for example, would be sufficient to kill off all humanity through respiratory paralysis. Actually, the poison existed by the gallon in all the arsenals, ready for use.

Jeanne continued her investigation in Washington, Denver, Houston and New York, always on her guard but never hiding or concealing what she was after. The small nucleus of highly trained people working in the fields of chemical and biological warfare was enveloped in a cloud of spies and counterspies who swirled around them like mosquitoes over a stagnant pond. Jeanne met them all and told them plainly that she was looking not for secrets, but for a man. She talked with scientists, scoundrels, swindlers, some with deliriously mad imaginations and others who were on the make and ready to invent any kind of wild information to sell to the highest bidder. The mixture of sensationalism and contradiction created a confusion that helped to hide the secret itself. Jeanne gradually became acquainted with most of the intelligence agents swarming around the Pentagon and its annexes, all of whom seemed to know each other well. She did not offer them any competition. She was not dangerous and she wrote out checks easily. So they willingly told her what they knew and invented what they didn't know, as long as she was willing to pay. But just because she was receiving information from all sides, she began to understand that this blind, antlike activity was ludicrous and futile, that all these agents and counteragents were only playing a game among themselves, none of them knowing one whit more than anyone else.

Once again she returned to Paris, exhausted and ill from viral hepatitis contracted while being given a series of calcium injections to help her keep going. While convalescing, she had the time to give serious thought to the

Lancet article and what it revealed about the work of
the Bombay laboratories—and indirectly that of Pavilion L. As soon as she was able to get about, she consulted the back editions of *Le Figaro* and *France-Soir*, the
French daily papers, to compare the details of the two
fires. But the French papers gave only very brief ac-
counts. The one thing she did discover of any interest
was that in both Paris and Bombay, there were no survi-
vors. But there was also no mention of corpses.

While rapidly going over the papers, she did find
something she was not looking for: a photograph of
Nehru on his visit to Paris twenty days before the Villejuif explosion. The *Lancet* article had said that the "la-
mented Bahanba" had been a personal friend of the Indian Prime Minister.

Jeanne saw no particular significance in this. It might
be simply a coincidence, but she had decided to examine
thoroughly all such coincidences, all possibilities, all
pretenses until she found the fact they were concealing.

Chapter 17

She began to write:

> Roland, I have been looking for you for an eterni-
> ty. And yet it seems just yesterday, just a moment
> ago, that I was in your arms. And suddenly you were
> no longer there. I was naked, flayed alive, tormented,
> alone.
>
> They told me that you were dead, as I watched the
> flames in which you burned. But I couldn't believe
> that. If you had been dead everything would have
> stopped, as when a film breaks down and the char-

acters become suddenly immobile, empty phantoms who have never lived. You can't be dead, because I still live.

During the first years of my search, I waited, hoped for a signal from you, however brief, however incomprehensible it might be. I would have understood, would have known what you wanted to say in even a simple line drawn on a piece of stray paper. If you had wanted to send it you would have succeeded, even if you had been shut up in a cement prison without doors or windows. If I haven't received a sign from you it means that you are voluntarily silent, separated from me in the heart of mystery that you refuse to disclose, a secret greater than your love.

Since you cannot come back to me, since you refuse to send for me, despite everything that stands between us it is I who must succeed in reaching you.

I love you as I did the first day, as I did the last day we were together, when Paris was so wet and stormy, do you remember? Outside was the deluge, and inside were we, locked in each other's arms, you within me.

I love you.

I am writing this letter which I then intend to burn, so that you will receive it across any space or barrier.

I am coming to you. I am coming. . . .

Chapter 18

Jeanne did not wait to be completely cured before setting out again. In Bombay, overcome by the heat, ill, determined, harassed by a thousand beggars, half of whom were dying of hunger and the other half faking, she slowly, agonizingly traced back through the labyrinth of faulty memory and lies to what remained of a true reconstruction of the facts. She received so many confused and irrelevant answers to her questions that it was impossible for her to distinguish the few nuggets of truth from the vast quantities of untruth.

When she first met the man who had driven Nehru from the Bombay airport to Shri Bahanba's laboratory, she was convinced that he was lying. The man had become a minor government employee, a customs official stamping the passports of travelers arriving by air. Extremely dignified, he refused to accept any sort of tip, and so she finally believed what he told her. The official version stated that Bahanba and his collaborators had perished in the laboratory fire nine days after Nehru's return. Since Nehru had been dead for two years, confirmation of that visit could only be obtained from secondary witnesses. After weeks of inquiry, Jeanne chanced upon the track of Nehru's pilot. He had retired and was traveling all over India on foot, going from temple to temple to pray, begging for rice. After several months, by a stroke of luck, she found him in a Hindu religious retreat, Shri Aurobindo, in Pondicherry. One evening, sitting lotus fashion under a tree, he broke his silence and spoke. He was a gray-haired, ageless-looking man, and his coal-black eyes were soft and peaceful. He was naked to the waist, his bones protruding under a thin layer of muscles molded by yoga postures. Yes, he had taken the Pandit to Bombay and flown him back to New Dalhi. In the months that followed, they had flown to New York, Moscow, Peking, London, Paris and Bonn, where Nehru had met with the heads of state. He also told her about the second plane that had accompanied them everywhere. He did not know who had been aboard.

And his eyes, the tone of his voice and his superb control over his body conveyed louder than words that all this was merely fruitless agitation, that the only voyage worth anything at all was motionless, into one's own inner self.

After so many years of confused and relentless search in every direction, after so many false scents, after so many right tracks thwarted, after persistence without results and results of no interest, the few phrases she heard in the tranquillity of that garden full of sleeping birds soothed Jeanne's aching soul. The names mentioned and the voyager who linked them together finally indicated a definite road on which she might advance. Before starting out on that road, she took her first rest. She remained at the religious retreat, building up her moral and physical forces, then returned to Bombay, where she now hoped to pinpoint the origin of the entire affair.

She discovered the name of an assistant biologist who had left the laboratory two months before the fire to take a position as a scientist with the government at New Delhi. Jeanne arrived in the capital and was soon buried in Indian administrative red tape. The profusion of bureaucrats was equaled only by their good will. She did not know exactly where to begin, so she explored the possibilities in those services dealing with science and public health. Nobody knew anything, but everybody tried to help her. One afternoon she asked the same question for the thousandth time, in this case to a man clad in a white summer suit and seated behind a small desk under a large fan. The man answered with a smile that the woman she was looking for was his own sister, that she worked in his department and that she was presently traveling throughout the countryside to publicize contraception.

Jeanne caught up with her the next day in a village about forty miles to the northwest of Calcutta. It was market day. The contraception team had set up a military tent in the marketplace. The tent was covered with simple brightly colored drawings representing scenes from the lives of the gods.

A number of young women and several men entered
the tent. The women came out wearing an *ogino* collar
to help them count their sterile days and their fertile
days. They were delighted, believing that it would be
sufficient to put the collar around their neck to avoid becoming pregnant. The men were offered transistor radi-
os in exchange for their voluntary sterilization. The surgeon operated on his patients immediately next door,
under a hospital tent marked with a red cross.

The peasants, seated in the shade of a banyan tree,
had spread out their fruits and vegetables on rags and
newspapers. Flies buzzed among the customers. Some
monkeys walked about among the buyers and the cows.
From time to time, one of them snatched a mango or a
radish, darted away shrieking as if it were being pursued
and climbed to the top of a roof to eat its spoils.

Chapter 19

The story told to Jeanne Corbet by the woman who
had been one of Shri Bahanba's lab assistants was a full
account of what had happened in the scientist's laboratory the day before Nehru's visit.

The young biologist was working that day, January
16, 1955, in the room next to that of Bahanba. At
around nine-thirty in the morning, she looked through
the glass partition and saw Bahanba's chief assistant
cover his eyes with his hand, then point toward a large
bouquet of flowers, a number of which he presently removed, flourished at Bahanba and finally placed on a table.

All the flowers were red.

The young woman saw Bahanba's face express a degree of agitation surprising in a man of such perfect serenity. He first quickly locked the laboratory door, shut the windows firmly, returned to his chief assistant, made him sit down, examined his eyes and the palms of his hands, than sat down himself and began to speak. The chief assistant's face expressed great surprise, then joy, then fear. At one point, as though to counter some objections that the young man seemed to be expressing, Bahanba arose and took a small glass container from a shelf. When he showed it to the chief assistant, the woman could see that it contained a living butterfly with brown wings and blue markings. The young man suddenly looked overwhelmed and dismayed.

Bahanba replaced the container on the shelf and remained erect and immobile for several minutes, his eyes closed, meditating. His chief assistant looked at him in silence. Bahanba opened his eyes, turned toward him and talked to him quietly and at length. The young man now seemed completely reassured and calm.

Picking up the telephone, Bahanba called each lab throughout the building and informed the personnel that, due to their work in progress, he and his chief assistant would have to remain in their laboratory night and day. For reasons that he could not disclose, he was obliged to interrupt temporarily the activities of the research center. He asked the researchers and staff to consider themselves on leave starting that very evening. He counted on the lab heads to take the necessary measures regarding the small animals and microbial cultures in the lab. Nobody, absolutely nobody, was to be permitted to enter the buildings as of the following morning.

They were all astonished, but the young biologist complied along with the others. She sacrificed a certain number of mice inoculated with tumors or infectious diseases, burning them in the incinerator. She didn't know what to do with the healthy ones. They were two gray mice and a white one. She remembered them well. Uncertain as to whether someone would remain in the lab to take care of them, she finally decided to set them free. She let them fall gently from the window into the grass below. Since they had been born and nurtured in cages, such an infinity of space caused them to huddle against the bottom of the wall. She tried to scare them away with gestures, but they refused to budge. They had certainly been eaten before dawn by the cats roaming in the garden if not by the mongooses, serpents or night birds.

She destroyed the bacterial cultures that might become dangerous and placed others in a freezer.

On her way out, she passed two servants carrying two camp beds, armchairs and food.

The following week, she received a dismissal notice along with her final salary and a sizable bonus. She found a government job and later learned of Bahanba's death in the newspapers.

She remembered these events in detail and was able to give Jeanne chapter and verse about Bahanba's research work at that time. It involved systematic and extensive study of substances or microorganisms capable of inducing the production in cells of antibodies against cancer. There was nothing especially singular about that. Other laboratories throughout the world were working on the same problem. She had noticed that for several months previously, Shri Bahanba had at times been extraordinarily grave and silent, like someone who must resolve a personal problem of extreme importance. She thought that he had arrived at a turning point in his spiritual evolution. No, he had not been ill. On the contrary, he seemed to be in better health than ever.

Chapter 20

In 1963, Samuel Frend was stationed at the Embassy in Mexico. During the month of May, he was called upon to deal with an American tourist who was trying to obtain a visa for Cuba and the U.S.S.R. via the Soviet Embassy in Mexico. The F.B.I. had classified him as an unimportant suspect, essentially "small potatoes." The visas he requested were refused, and he returned to the United States. Several months later, on November 22, in Dallas, he became infamous throughout the world. His name was Lee Harvey Oswald.

Frend would not have attached any importance to him, but during the last days of Oswald's stay in Mexico, he was seen in the company of someone Frend had already met several times in Paris at the time of the Villejuif fire and again during the summit conference between Eisenhower, Khrushchev, Macmillan and de Gaulle. Frend knew this man under three aliases, but he had given him a fourth: he called him "Summer" in his reports, because he had had dealings with him for the first time on June 21 in Warsaw.

With his small, protruding belly, smiling, round face and rosy, bald pate surrounded by white hair, Summer resembled a minor character in an American comedy. His clothes were ill-fitting, and he gave the impression of being a nice grandpa with candy in his pockets to be doled out to the little ones. In fact, he was one of the most dangerous men in the world, ever ready to arrange theft, murder, kidnapping, scandal. He indiscriminately hired himself out to East or West or to individuals. Even

57

the Mafia sometimes called on him, though he never actually belonged to that organization. His services came high, but the results justified his prices.

Frend had been susprised to see him prowling around Villejuif at the time of the events of 1955. If he had not seen the work of Colonel P.'s men with his own eyes, he would doubtless have attributed the fire to Summer.

During the Paris conference of 1960, the Pentagon, which continued to look upon Eisenhower as a general rather than as the President of the United States, was extremely worried about his security. The military services had no confidence in the F.B.I. nor in the Secret Service. They surrounded the President with their own men and saw to it that Samuel Frend preceded him to Paris. Frend had been chosen to be responsible for making the terrain safe because of his considerable familiarity with the French capital.

He arrived three months before the opening of the conference and installed himself on the Champs-Elysées in the offices of a film company. Plunging into the Parisian atmosphere with nostalgic joy, he renewed his old contacts and established new ones. He met with agents of all allegiances or none at all, who were absolutely determined to discover, transmit, interpret, develop, efface, falsify, buy, sell all that was said or not said, whispered or shouted in the corridors of the conference. Every secret agreement or dissent, every intention or reservation of those meetings became subject to exhaustive scrutiny.

An important conference is an occasion for subtle satisfaction for top diplomats and promotion for lesser ones, as well as a veritable windfall for secret-service agents. Each of them in turn, depending on his rank or skill, extracts his pound of flesh, leaving yet one more skeleton on the great desert of international detente.

At Frend's instigation, the American Embassy asked the French police to arrest several small operators of no importance, a measure calculated to justify his own presence in Paris rather than to allay his fear for the President's safety. On May 2, he bought a strange piece of information from a German agent who had obtained it by sharing a bed with a homosexual Rumanian diplomat: Khrushchev was carrying to Paris an object to which he attached so much value that he kept it with him constantly in the inside pocket of his jacket. His rivals at the Kremlin had vainly attempted to have it stolen from him. Three fruitless attempts had provoked Khrushchev's terrible anger. It was not known whether those who had tried to gain possession of the object knew exactly what it was or simply were aware of its importance

On May 5, through one of his contacts, Frend received an invitation from a certain "Mr. Smith" to lunch at the Grand Vefour restaurant. As he approached the table, Frend recognized Summer. They ate a superlative meal washed down with an unforgettable wine. The weather was exquisite. The pigeons in the Palais Royal flew under the covered gallery and were reflected in the mirrors on the ceiling of the restaurant. Mr. Smith offered to sell to Frend for the sum of half a million dollars an extremely important object that the Russian leader always carried with him in the pocket of his jacket.

Frend did not doubt for an instant Mr. Smith's ability to steal the object so important to the Russian leader. It would require the mobilization of ten or fifteen of the best pickpockets in the world, spreading them around in different spots, then provoking an incident, a public disturbance of some kind, even, if necessary, a riot, to give one of them the chance to approach close enough to Khrushchev to act. "Smith" had probably organized the whole affair already. But Frend tried to learn more about the object itself. Mr. Smith could not tell him, as he knew nothing. Frend believed him, certain that if

"Smith" had known, he would have profited from that knowledge by raising his fee.

Frend declared that he did not have such a sum of money at his disposition and that he must transfer the offer to a higher echelon. Mr. Smith granted a delay of two days before the offer would be made elsewhere. They agreed to meet at the end of the two days at the same table.

Actually, Frend did have a sufficiently large budget to make the deal. But, though the offer interested him enormously, it was none of his concern since the object in question was certainly not a weapon with which Khrushchev proposed to make an attempt on Eisenhower's life. And Frend's mission in Paris consisted exclusively of watching over Eisenhower's safety. Therefore, he passed on the offer to one of his colleagues at the Embassy. Five months previously, three microphones had been secretly installed in the latter's office to monitor what took place there. They transmitted everything that was said into a tape recorder concealed in a locked metal safe in an office on the floor above. It belonged to an American government official who had been maneuvered by Colonel P.'s services into working for them.

Colonel P., who had passed from the employ of President Coty to that of President de Gaulle, was informed the very same night of Mr. Smith's proposal to the Americans, and he in turn informed General de Gaulle. The latter ordered him to stop the theft at all costs. Let Khrushchev be robbed elsewhere. De Gaulle ordered that no scandal would occur in Paris during the conference.

Two days later, while eating hors d'oeuvres, Frend announced to Mr. Smith that his offer had been accepted and to close the deal gave him on account a certified check for half a million Swiss francs made out to the bearer on a bank in Lausanne.

At a neighboring table, a bald man was eating asparagus. Mr. Smith remarked that it was peculiar to eat something cooked simply in water in Raymond Oliver's famed restaurant. Smiling voluptuously, he leaned over his chicken with lobster sauce. Melting with happiness at the third mouthful, he let himself go and as a bonus told Frend some of his latest discoveries. He still didn't know the nature of the object in Mr. Khrushchev's pocket, but he suspected that it was somehow related to the fire at Villejuif, the destruction of the biologist Bahanba's laboratory at Bombay and the fact that the Queen of England never let her pocketbook out of her hands.

Eisenhower and de Gaulle certainly knew what it was all about, and probably Macmillan too. And the Paris conference undoubtedly had a secret raison d'être infinitely more important than its declared one.

Now that Mr. Smith suspected all this, he regretted not having asked for more money, but a deal was a deal, and he would not go back on his demands. The two then came to an agreement about how the object was to be delivered and the final payment made.

Khrushchev arrived in Paris on May 14 and slept at the Soviet Embassy, protected by bulletproof doors and Russian police. The next morning at breakfast, the Russian leader noticed that the leather case, smaller than a package of cigarettes, which never left the inside pocket of his jacket, was no longer there.

His rage shook the walls of the Embassy. He ordered that everyone and everything in the Embassy be closely examined and searched the ambassador himself but found nothing. He recalled that the evening before, while undressing, he had forgotten to verify that the case was still in his pocket. And during the day, he had walked around Paris, shook hands, had even gone into a small grocery shop on the rue de Bourgogne near the Embassy. He had spoken with the salesgirls, bought some fruit, joked with everyone.

He decided that he must have been robbed there by

one of the British or American agents who had accompanied Eisenhower and Macmillan to Paris. They would pay dearly for it.

On the morning of the sixteenth, at the first session, Khrushchev broke up the conference, using as a pretext the fact that an American reconnaissance plane had been shot down over the U.S.S.R. It was obviously only a lame excuse, since from 1956 on, these planes had been flying at an altitude high enough to escape being caught over the Soviet Union, and Khrushchev and the other Soviet authorities were perfectly aware of this. Furthermore, the shooting down of a reconnaissance plane and the perfecting of an antiaircraft missile, making it impossible for these flights to continue, constituted a victory of sorts and should have filled Khrushchev with satisfaction and pride. His humiliation and rage, which he could barely contain before the journalists, was certainly due to another reason, a reason that Eisenhower knew nothing about, that Macmillan did not suspect (Mr. Smith was wrong in thinking that they were in on the secret), but that de Gaulle guessed immediately. De Gaulle confirmed his hunch several hours later when he had time to summon Colonel P.

At three P.M. on May 17, Frend, who had also guessed the reasons for Khrushchev's outburst, stopped his car in the Parc de Saint-Cloud and awaited Mr. Smith, who had promised to deliver the famous object to him. Mr. Smith did not appear that day nor the next, nor in the week that followed. And Frend, whose mission was ended, returned to the United States convinced that Mr. Smith had finally decided to sell the object at a higher price elsewhere. One always had to be prepared to expect everything of anybody in this business.

At five P.M. on May 16, de Gaulle was finaly able to retire to his office and receive Colonel P. He coldly asked if he had followed instructions and protected the

Russian leader against any robbery attempt. Colonel P. declared that his men had not left Khrushchev alone for a second. As soon as he had set foot from the Soviet Embassy, they had accompanied him everywhere, along with the Soviet bodyguards, the French police and French Secret Service agents. Khrushchev had floated around Paris like a star surrounded by a flotilla of satellites both visible and invisible. None of them had noticed anything unusual.

Another group had kept an eye on Mr. Smith. He had not been out of their sight for one second, even when he was in his apartment at the Ritz. He had never even been anywhere near Khrushchev. The events of the morning, however, had made the Colonel fear that something had happened, and so he had acted with a brutality and lack of tact for which he felt he should excuse himself, but there are moments when . . .

"That's all right," said de Gaulle. "Continue."

"I went personally to the Ritz with my best men and arrested Smith. I ransacked his apartment and opened his safe. He protested, called his lawyer and his ambassador."

"Which one?"

"The British ambassador, General."

"And did the ambassador send someone?"

"He came himself. I didn't let him in. I had Smith taken to the prison at Vincennes, where he is being held in a secret cell guarded by two of my men. I've brought you the only objects that seemed to be of any interest. Personally, I don't see anything that justifies or explains Khrushchev's anger."

"Show them to me," de Gaulle ordered.

Colonel P. opened his briefcase and placed before the General a miniature walkie-talkie hidden in a package of Marlboro cigarettes, an electronic thumb-sized Japanese doll that talked and walked, a small roll of tape recordings, three tiny microphones, a notebook filled with code words and a red leather case that might have contained a wristwatch.

De Gaulle examined everything, then picked up the case and opened it. A label was attached to the object that it contained. Three Cyrillic letters were written by hand on the label. De Gaulle had learned a bit of Russian in preparation for a state visit to Eastern Europe, and so he immediately recognized what was meant by the three letters, one of which signified a number. He closed the red case and replaced it on the table among the other objects.

"General, would you give me full power to interrogate Smith?"

"Not worth it. Deport him. Put him on a plane that will take him as far away as possible. Make your excuses to the British ambassador. And remove these odds and ends."

But when Colonel P. had taken back the microphones, the notebook, the doll and the tapes, and was reaching for the red case, de Gaulle said, "No, leave that with me!"

He thought over how, by failing to protect Khrushchev from being robbed and by behaving at the Ritz like a country policeman, Colonel P. had doubtless spared the West and the rest of the world an unimaginable adventure. But he had done it in spite of himself, through an error. Stupid, like most military men, he deserved to be both punished and rewarded. De Gaulle decided to put him on the retirement list, but only after having promoted him to the rank of general.

On July 17, 1960, Samuel Frend, on vacation in Minneapolis, received a letter from Mr. Smith explaining his failure to deliver the promised merchandise. He did not like breaking his word, thus earning a reputation for unreliability.

I am sorry to inform you that Colonel P., whom you knew well, died in an automobile accident yesterday afternoon near Chambéry. The merchandise I was to deliver to you is now in hands of his immediate superior. It is inaccessible to me. Therefore, I must consider this affair to be terminated—unhappily, not in the way we would have wished. I hope this will not prevent you from having confidence in me for some future dealings. I assume that you do not expect me to reimburse the deposit you paid. It has not even covered my expenses.

It was this same Mr. Smith whom Frend, to his great surprise, saw talking with the insignificant Lee Oswald on May 13, 1963, in Mexico. He was informed by the C.I.A. about another meeting between the two but did not have time to arrange for monitoring it. Smith returned to Europe and Oswald to the United States before Frend was able to discover what bargain had been concluded between the two.

He notified the F.B.I. of the encounter, and it was duly entered in Oswald's record. But this was not enough to cause any particular surveillance of Oswald during President Kenndey's visit to Dallas. From a window on the sixth floor of the Texas School Book Depository, Oswald was able to calmly fire on the President.

Frend was horror-stricken by the assassination of a man he so admired. Thinking that perhaps he held one of the threads that would lead to the real instigators of Kennedy's murder, Frend reminded his superiors of the Smith-Oswald meetings in Mexico. When he asked for authorization to start an investigation in that direction, the Pentagon's answer was negative. Frend took an unlimited leave of absence and left for Dallas, where he made a personal investigation. He found indisputable evidence of Mr. Smith's visit there and acquired the conviction if not the proof that Smith had organized not only Kennedy's assassination by Oswald but also that of

Oswald by Ruby. Frend sent report after report to his superiors but received no reaction whatsoever. Neither the Pentagon nor the F.B.I. showed any interest in these reports, the Pentagon because the affair was not in its bailiwick and the F.B.I. because of the millions of unverifiable denunciations and explanations they received, so that they relied only on established facts.

As a last resort, Frend sent a report to President Johnson himself, declaring that he believed President Kennedy's death to be linked with the sabotage of the Paris conference and other inexplicable events he described therein.

Eight days later, Frend, who had returned to his job at the Embassy in Mexico, received a personal letter from President Johnson inviting him to the White House on the following day. Frend took a plane directly to Washington. A White House car was awaiting him at the airport. He got in, the car drove off, and neither arrived at the White House.

Investigating his father's disappearance several months later, Samuel Frend's eldest son was told by the Presidential staff that no car had been sent to the airport that day from the White House.

Chapter 21

Paul Corbet received a final letter from his wife on May 17, 1972. During the course of 1971, Jeanne Corbet's investigations had led her to the conviction that only several heads of state were aware of the great secret. President Pompidou knew nothing, as Jeanne had ascertained during an interview with him. He had seemed intrigued by two or three questions she had asked, but undoubtedly, on thinking it over, had believed her to be slightly deranged.

Her Majesty Elizabeth II had politely refused to receive her a second time.

Paul Corbet had treated ex-President Johnson's heart condition several years earlier, and so his request that Jeanne be allowed to visit the Johnson ranch in Texas was accepted.

This is the letter Jeanne wrote to her husband:

Paul, we will never see each other again. I have reached the end of my quest. President Johnson was extremely alarmed when I began to question him and he realized how much I knew. He declared that he himself knew of nothing he could tell me, but he telephoned in my presence to President Nixon and arranged an immediate rendezvous. I slept at the ranch. It's an extraordinary place, but I didn't really have the time nor the inclination to really look at it. The next day a helicopter took me to an airport, but I don't know which one. I was received by two young men who seemed to be military officers dressed in civilian clothes. We flew to Washington in a Boeing in which we were the only passengers. These two men accompanied me to the White House where I was received by President Nixon. He was pleasant and cordial, knew all about my search, and smiled as he told me that he had never before encountered such a determined woman. Then he became serious and said: "Determined and finally dangerous." He repeated the word "dangerous" and then suddenly asked: "Do you want to join your friend?" I was so choked with emotion that I couldn't answer. He added: "But if you do and decide to go where he is, you will never come back." I finally was able to say "Yes, I want to with all my heart." And that is it. I know nothing more. I am alone in a small room at the White House. They are coming in a moment to take me I don't know where. I asked if I might write you a note. The President said he would personally see to

it that it reaches you. In a few minutes I shall be
leaving to meet Roland and I will never see you
again. I feel no remorse because after all this is what
you wanted for me too. But I am sorry, as you must
know, because despite my happiness I hate the idea
of losing you. You will know what to say to Nicolas.
He hasn't needed me for ages and he adores you. I
think he will be happy if he marries Suzanne. I hope
this letter reaches you, but even though I have no
secret to betray, since I don't really know anything,
I am afraid that I have written too much as it is. I
beg the person or persons reading these lines to decide
if they should be sent to you and at least let me tell
you how grateful I am and how much I do love and
respect you. Jeanne.

While Jeanne was leaving the White House with the
two U.S. Air Force officers in mufti who had accompanied her, President Nixon read with some difficulty the
letter she had given him for Paul. His knowledge of
French was fragmentary, but he couldn't entrust it to a
translator. He read it again and again, cutting out most
of it and burning the potenitally dangerous words in an
ashtray, then gave the rest to his secretary to mail.

Chapter 22

During the latter half of the 1960s, certain scientists and technicians from the most disparate nations disappeared.

At Meudon, France, Eugene Libert, an astronomer
who was riding home on his bicycle on September 7,
1966, after a night spent at the observatory, never arrived at his destination.

In Detroit, on March 3, 1967, Albury King, a chemist and specialist in steel alloys, was last seen getting on a bus for Ann Arbor. There was no known reason for him to go there, and in fact he never arrived at that destination.

On August 29, 1969, the Dutch biologist L. Groning, the only man in the world to have succeeded in maintaining a champanzee alive in subzero tempreature, disappeared while en route to Yugoslavia via Western Germany.

Also listed as having disappeared or died in accidents were an American engineer working for N.A.S.A. in perfectioning solar cells, a German horticulturist, an entire group of Russians doing research on the nature of gravity, a Swiss hotel man, two architects, some skilled workers. The list contained a hundred or more persons, men and women, each at the top of his professional specialty. The Japanese physicist Kinoshita, dying of cancer, was taken out of the hospital by his family even though he supposedly had only a few days left to live. The coffin that was lowered into his grave a week later actually contained only a sack of earth.

Since tens of thousands of people disappear each year and are never found, these bizarre occurrences did not attract any particular attention.

Eleven days after Jeanne Corbet's visit to the White House, her husband received by mail two fragments of paper that had been cut by a pair of scissors from a larger sheet. He read:

In a few minutes I shall be leaving to meet Roland and I will never see you again . . . how grateful I am and how much I do love and respect you. Jeanne.

On June 22, 1972, while the eminent cardiologist was walking in his garden on the rue de Varenne after breakfast, he had a heart attack and died on the spot, at the age of seventy-three.

Nicolas, the son of Paul and Jeanne, married. He and his wife, Suzanne, are both doctors. Nicolas was not endowed with his father's genius, but he has a determined nature like his mother. He believes that she died in the United States of an intestinal hemorrhage. A death certificate to this effect arrived with an urn containing ashes in July, 1972.

Chapter 23

The Aleutian Islands are the peaks of a long chain of mountains that jut out of the sea and form an invisible arch connecting Alaska and the Soviet Union. This submerged dike between America and Asia raises a colossal barrier between the warm waters of the Pacific and the icy Arctic seas that have managed to slip through the Bering Strait.

The Aleutians are situated at approximately the same latitude as England and Newfoundland. In the month of June, the days are interminable and bright. The mist, lit from above by the perpetually shining sun, covers the water and the land like a mantle. Overhead, seabirds wail without end, like lost dogs trying to find their way home.

Jeanne's plane had been waiting five days at a military base in Alaska for an improvement in the weather that would enable them to take off. She knew neither where she was nor where she was going. She had not been permitted to leave the plane, which had no portholes. All she could hear were the whistling of the wind and the roar of the motors of incoming and outgoing planes. Her meals were served to her and all her wishes granted, insofar as possible, by a kindly but rather irascible sergeant who had taken charge six days earlier at the secret military air field where she had been given a one-month training course as a parachutist. It was a simple transport plane and therefore not very comfortable, its rear section consisting of a berth and somewhat primitive toilet facilities.

Jeanne had asked the sergeant several questions. First of all, his name. He had answered, 'My name is Walter. You can call me Walt."

What were they waiting for? "Weather report. . . ."

Where were they, where were they going? With obvious satisfaction and pride, he had replied, "Military secret!" He was pleased not to be allowed to say anything and still more pleased not really to know anything. As it turned out, his job was to help Jeanne make her leap when he received the signal to do so. That was all he needed or wanted to know.

Finally, on Tuesday morning, he announced that the weather report was favorable and that they were doubtless going to take off. An hour later, he returned and declared that their departure was imminent. He fastened the door; the engines began to roar, then suddenly stopped. The telephone communicating with the cockpit began to jingle, a light flashed. Walt lifted the receiver, said "Yes," listened, said "Well," then hung up.

"Countermanded," he told Jeanne. "Have to wait."

"Wait for what?"

"Just wait."

He was a soldier and therefore accustomed to changes in orders. He sat down and nonchalantly began to eat a sandwich. Jeanne tried to remain calm but found herself unable to eat.

Toward eleven o'clock, the telephone rang once more,

and again Walt took up the receiver, again said "Yes," "Well," then hung up.

He turned to Jeanne and announced, "We're leaving," just as the engines began to turn. A quarter of an hour later, the plane sped along the runway as if chased by dogs from hell.

Having reached the specified altitude, it headed for Islet 307.

The islet was located almost at the pinnacle of the archipelago, toward the arch of the chain of undersea mountains. When the sky was blue, the sound of foghorns and sirens ceased, and the warships on guard around the islet withdrew to their maximum prescribed limits. These American warships were spread out into three concentric circles. When the visibility was good, the three circles of ships turned slowly around the islet, the first two in clockwise fashion, the third, composed of the fastest crafts, in the opposite direction. When the fog was heavy, as frequently occurred, the three circles converged and slackened speed, steering by radar with all sirens screaming. Collisions were frequent but generally not serious.

D. H. Kemplin was the admiral in charge, He had taken command on March 1 and hoped to be relieved very soon, as he found the perpetual nervous tension and the terribly empty monotony of his task almost unendurable. The orders, proceeding directly from the President of the United States and issued to all the unit commanders, were to shoot down, after proper warning, any person crossing the double network of red buoys that surrounded the island. These buoys, located about 100 yards offshore, were equipped with radar, sonar and infrared mine detectors. Some of the ships were armed with powerful, long-range flamethrowers. The orders were to destroy not only anyone leaving the Island but also his craft and all its contents. The two picket ships patrolling among the three circles of ships carried a cannon-laser capable of atomizing the sea at its point of impact, raising its heat to 3,000 degrees. Helicopters circled the buoys twenty-four hours a day, whatever the weather. They were loaded with napalm that was to be used in an emergency.

The admiral thought that he was responsible for the security of an ultrasecret miltary center for atomic research. The officers and sailors of the fleet, and all those stationed elsewhere who knew about the existence of Islet 307 and its special situation, believed the same. In fact, it was in the depths of this islet that the subterranean explosion, canceled by Eisenhower after Nehru's visit, was to have taken place. The various crews were convinced that scientists were preparing a new bomb there that would reduce the H-bomb to the rank of a firecracker.

From time to time, two or three Soviet trawlers would approach the American ships without bothering to camouflage their maneuvers from the ultramodern detection devices of the fleet. Several times, the fleet even saw a large Chinese junk arrive, a kind of astonishing fishing boat equipped with sails and motors, which appeared to be something other than it seemed because of the way it withstood stormy weather of the worst sort. These strange craft were at once reported to Washington from where the order immediately came not to pay any attention to them.

No serious attempt had ever been made to pass through the buoys to gain the open sea. However, in fine weather, one or two or even a flotilla of white barges capped with a sort of cover that made them absolutely airtight could be seen coming from a channel that entered a tunnel. The covering was transparent but polarized, thus making it impossible to see what was inside. These boats frolicked over the water like a flock of white ducks, coming and going in all directions, turning about, encircling the Island, but only on two occasions did one of them try to pass beyond the first line of buoys, and this inadvertently, rather than intending to reach the open sea. At the first warning from the Admiral's amplifiers, the boat returned to the authorized zone.

The fleet had been guarding the Island for seventeen years against a danger that seemed to be nonexistent. Nothing ever happened, but constant training exercises kept the crews from becoming inattentive and careless. An occasional collision between ships meeting in the mist created an incident that helped the sailors to release their nervous energy.

On this Tuesday morning, when Admiral Kemplin at last saw the week-old mist lift, he sighed with relief and immediately boarded a transport that had been waiting for some days to unload its cargo. The transport had arrived on the preceding Friday in a thick pea-soup fog.

The ship faced the Island, approached as close as possible to the buoys, then stopped. This was the usual procedure. On the Island, the entrance gate into the hill opened.

The Admiral looked once more at the land in the hope of at last perceiving something unusual there. Seen from the gangway of the transport ship, the Island appeared to be a small, rocky plateau dominated in the center by a double-peaked gray hill, the outline of which suggested a camel's back. The two humps of the camel had been joined before 1955 by a cement mass intended to be both a superstructure for the subterranean installations and living quarters for the members of the atomic mission. Perhaps, due to the thickness of its concrete, it also served as a bulwark against accidental radiation leaks and even as a test of resistance against explosion.

Admiral Kemplin, who had served as a young officer in Algeria, found that, viewed from the west, this construction, firmly implanted on both sides into the rocks of the two humps, resembled a small, very compact Arab town. It formed a disorderly but harmonious compound of cubes and spheres interposed one on top of the other, with no streets, doors or windows, reaching to the height of the summit of the hill. The only visible opening, large enough to let trucks pass through it three abreast, was located at the foot of the northern hump, facing west. It was closed by a cement block rolled along on rails that was used to make the entrance narrower or wider as needed. A broad asphalt road led from this entrance gate to the small port constructed on a rocky point that was sheltered from the northern winds. To the south of the port stretched a black gravel beach on which an old landing barge lay stranded.

The concrete block slipped aside to open the entrance to the hill, and the usual convoy of trucks and jeeps and cranes passed out and headed toward the beach. These brightly painted vehicles were, as always, streaming wet, as though they had emerged from the sea. They were driven by men in white, airtight flying suits topped by transparent, spherical helmets equipped with self-contained breathing apparatuses.

The front of the waiting transport ship was lowered like a drawbridge, and a huge, flat-bottomed, inflatable barge loaded with soldered metal cases of every dimension was rolled down to the sea. Nobody was on board. With its motor running and its rudder set in the direction of the Island, the barge edged through the buoys and sped toward the shore. It grounded with a crashing sound upon the beach, where the men in white were awaiting it. One crane hoisted it onto dry land, and another began transferring its load to a truck. Like all the vehicles on the Island, these cranes functioned silently, no doubt due to electric motors. Or perhaps, Kemplin supposed, atomic ones.

Giving it no further thought, he slapped his face and neck with his gloved hands. Mosquitoes were the scourge of the Aleutian summer.

Two other barges had followed the first one. Men

from the Island were now busy unloading them, much like white ants cutting up June bugs before carrying the pieces into the depths of their anthill. From time to time, one of the men would stop and give a friendly wave of the hand to the transport, and the sailors would respond with similar gestures of good fellowship. The front of the transport slowly closed up. The three empty barges would not be taken back on board. Instead, they would be deflated and transported to the interior of what the officers and their men were accustomed to calling the Citadel. Nothing ever came back from the Island.

The transport made a half-turn and headed south, while the launch that had brought the Admiral from the flagship was now heading north, taking him back around the Island.

The far end of the hill dipped straight down into the sea, the depth at this point being approximately two thousand yards. At a hundred yards above the water, a kind of gutter protruded from the wall of rock; it was a crater, in fact, since it ejected only highly heated refuse and shapeless matter that, at the end of its long fall, was still hot enough to turn the water to a boil. Its path had traced a black streak down the hill.

In the month of January, 1969, in the course of a short winter's day, a sailor looking at the Island through field glasses had seen the great door of the hill open and a child come out. She was a small girl, as far as he could make out, entirely naked and golden brown, as though toasted by the Florida sun, with long, ash-blond hair and small budding nipples.

She came running outside for a moment, then stopped, raised her face and then her hands toward the sky and began a sort of joyful little dance. Two men came quickly from the Citadel and led the child back inside. Laughing, she let them take her.

Chapter 24

On November 22, 1963, when Vice President Lyndon Johnson took his oath of office in the Presidential plane at Dallas, he was aware of the existence of Islet 307 and the perpetual guard set up around it. But he too believed this to be some secret matter involving purely military activities. And Kennedy, given the circumstances of his death, had been unable to disabuse Johnson and pass on to him the burden of the truth.

The day after Johnson's installation in office, the head of the White House Secret Service revealed to him the location of a safe securely hidden away in his office and whose combination was unknown. Several days later, two generals, two senators and the Chief Justice of the Supreme Court each brought him an envelope they had received from Kennedy with the confidential orders that if he were to die in a sudden manner before the end of his term, it was to be passed on to his successor. None of these people knew that this mission had been given to the others. As a result, Lyndon Johnson found himself with five letters, each containing a serial number permitting him to construct the combination of the safe. He opened the safe and found a notebook full of figures in Kennedy's handwriting. A few lines on the first page stated that the code for the message would be delivered to him in the form of a book sent by a woman who would use only her first name in signing it.

Among the messages of sympathy and good wishes that Johnson received from the chiefs of state, there was one given to him by the British ambassador on behalf of his sovereign. The message was signed by Queen Elizabeth and accompanied by a Douay Version of the Bible. At first, the President did not understand, and then an intriguing thought occurred to him. He tried and found that the Bible was indeed the key.

The code message was composed of groups of three numbers. The first designated the page, the second the row of the line starting from the top, the third the order of the word in the line. This was the most classic and simplest of all the codes, but also the most difficult to decipher, since one had to know what book held the key and how to use it. Only ten copies of this particular English edition of the Douay Version, printed in Spain during the eighteenth century, were still extant. Kennedy had owned one, which his widow had taken away along with all his personal belongings at the time of his death.

Evening after evening, President Johnson worked at decoding the message. It was comparatively brief, but to search for individual words in such a large book was a long and tedious task. Also, he had limited time to work on it because of his official duties. When he finally discovered what the full message contained, he passed a sleepless night and, by morning, had lost his previous somewhat naïve optimism. The problem distressed him, haunted his thoughts night and day amidst all his other burdens. When he gave up his candidacy for the Presidency, it was not only because of Vietnam but also because he no longer felt capable of bearing the responsibility of his knowledge of the greatest peril and the greatest hope the world had ever known.

Islet 307 was the permanent objective at which one Chinese, two American and two Russian atomic rockets were directed.

Chapter 25

"Do we still have far to go?" Jeanne asked.

"I don't know," Walt replied.

He handed her a cold hamburger spread with mustard. She thanked him with a smile but refused to take it. After struggling so long against barriers and pitfalls of every sort, she now had a sense of great sunlit peace, of profound, untroubled well-being. It was all over, the battle had been won. She would arrive in five minutes, or in five hours, to reap the fruits of her victory.

When she had first learned that she was finally to rejoin Roland, it had been so sudden that she had almost lost her equilibrium. The early hours that she had passed at an unknown military base, after her visit to the White House, now seemed to her quite mad. She had laughed, sobbed, tossed to and fro on her bed, talked to herself, to Roland, trying to convince him, to convince herself, that this great battle to end their separation was truly over and that they would soon be united forever.

Then fear had assailed her. She had suddenly realized how much she had changed physically over these years. Her long struggle had made of her a hard, unfeeling fighter. In contrast to many women, who became more generously round and full with age, she had the impression of having shrunk, of the soft folds of flesh around her bones having turned to tough muscle, and she saw the tiny dry wrinkles around her eyes and mouth. She had lost the gentle curves and graceful movements that make a woman so charming to a man in love.

Seized with panic in the middle of the night, she rose

from her bed and hurried to the washstand. The mirror was just large enough to permit a soldier to see his cheeks and his chin when he shaves. Jeanne stared at herself closely, then mounted a chair and twisted to try to see herself from the back; what she could not see, she tested with her hands.

The shoulders, still straight, were beautiful enough, with no thickening yet at the base of the neck. But the collarbones stuck out like the ribs of a hungry child.

Her breasts? Alas for her, her round and tilted breasts, which he had loved so much, had lost their firmness. And yet at least they didn't hang down, had never been large enough for that. She straightened up, raised her arms and saw in the mirror the bosom of an old maid. She continued her inventory, pleased to note her smooth, flat stomach, her long thighs, then her buttocks, like that of a boy—no, like that of an old bachelor! She was now fifty-three.

She threw herself on the bed and began to sob. Then she became calm, smiled, even began to laugh. Time had passed for Roland too. He would soon be fifty years old. Perhaps he had become the classic French middle-aged gentleman with a round belly and a pink bald head. She laughed harder and harder. Whatever he had become, she would always see him as handsome. She was coming to him after years of trials and illnesses, of courage and determination. However different she might look, inwardly nothing had changed. He would recognize her as she would recognize him, even if he had become very old indeed, one-eyed, legless. From the very first moment, they would know each other again as if they had left each other but the day before. They were going to have so very many things to tell each other until that gulf of years was closed, were it to take the rest of their lives. But now at least they could live together peacefully, hand in hand, all physical blemishes forgotten. She fell asleep.

A lamp suddenly lit up near the telephone. Walt grumbled, "Here we go." He got up and went to open the door. He hooked the parachute strap, which Jeanne had worn since the takeoff, to the cable on the roof of the cabin. He led Jeanne to the opening. The lamp sputtered. Walt cried, "Go!" and put out his hand to push her, but she had already jumped.

Chapter 26

Jeanne landed, rolled along as she had been taught to do, unhooked the red and blue parachute, stood up, removed her helmet, spat out a pebble and looked about her. She found herself on a gray beach; the sea was blue, the air hot and humid. Two warships were slowly moving about. The plane that had brought her banked its wings above them, the drone of its engines the only sound to mingle with that of the breaking of the small waves on the beach. On her left, a huge crab was scurrying along the hulk of an empty, rusty barge. It found a shadowy hole in a heap of old iron into which it sidled backward.

Jeanne turned and saw, between the two humps of the hill, the white Citadel outlined against the blue sky. Between the hill and the sea stretched a desert of gray rocks cut by the paler streak of the road and a short airplane runway. Not a tree, not a blade of grass, not a human being was visible. A few steps away, an empty bright-yellow jeep seemed to be waiting for her. She had the eerie impression of having dropped into a world painted by Dali or de Chirico. She didn't move. At that

moment, a voice that seemed to come from the jeep
spoke to her.

"Jeanne!"

Roland's voice! She shouted, "Yes."

"I'm delighted. Get into the jeep. There's only one
pedal. It's easy, you'll see. You bear down on the pedal,
it starts. You lift your foot, it stops. Gather up your parachute and put it into the jeep. Don't leave anything behind. You understand? Fine. Go along the road toward
the big gate. It will open. Don't get down from the jeep.
Go right in."

Chapter 27

The great cement gate opened and then closed behind her with a muffled thud. She lifted her foot, and the
jeep stopped. She was now in a large hall of white-
washed rough concrete built along the slender lines of a
Gothic cathedral. The hall was flooded with indirect
light. On the back wall, facing her above a closed copper door, a reversal of Dante's verse was painted in several colors and several languages:

ALL YOU WHO ENTER HERE
BE FILLED WITH HOPE

"Come, I'm waiting for you." It was Roland's gentle
voice.

The copper door opened.

Jeanne stepped from the jeep, looking nervously
around for a mirror to give a final touch to her hair; she
was hideous, she was sure of it, tired, messy, a fright.

Oh well, what of it! She smoothed her short hair, took three long strides and passed through the door. She could feel and even hear her rapid heartbeats.

She found herself in a sort of imitation drawing room done up in a mad turn-of-the-century style. Scrolls of lilies and twining roses were painted on the walls, framing the mirrors and the few pieces of military furniture, these too disguised in the style of the "belle époque." The fur of an immense white polar bear was stretched over the floor, partly concealing the cement.

The room was empty.

Jeanne's enthusiasm was cut short. Almost in a wail, she cried out, "Roland, where are you?"

"I'm here. I see you."

"Do you think that's fair, to look at me and not let me see you?"

She hid her face in her hands to cover its embarrassing nakedness.

"I'm sorry, dear. I had to prepare you before appearing. I wanted to see you first."

She heard a long sigh that seemed to fill the room with all the immense sadness a human heart can feel before the absurdity and injustice of the world. Roland's voice, low, hesitant, almost guilty, resumed:

"You are going to be very surprised—unpleasantly so, I'm afraid."

All the old fears that had assailed her during the long years of her search returned. What terrible illness had struck these people living at the end of the world in an isolation that hinted at something worse than leprosy?

"Roland!"

She controlled her emotions, took a deep breath and spoke calmly, without a quaver in her voice.

"You know that I love you. And no matter what has happened to you——"

Roland's voice interrupted her.

"No, no. It's not what you think. Prepare yourself for a shock. I'm coming."

She heard a door open on her left. She turned and faced it. A section of the wall revolved and Roland entered.

All the anguish of her long wait came to an end at that moment, and she was suffused with joy. Roland in good health. Roland untouched and whole. Roland handsome and resplendent. Roland just as she had left him.

Tears streaming down her face, she threw herself into his arms. Roland!

And then, suddenly, she began to realize what her eyes had just seen. *Roland stood before her just as she had left him!*

She drew back, looked at him again, then peered at the mirror on the wall. Through the lilies and roses, she saw a ridiculous, teary-eyed, disfigured old woman standing at the side of a superb man, radiant with youth. *Just as she had left him!* This was the image she had guarded intact in her memory over the years. But the seventeen years that had passed showed in ever line of her face and body, while *Roland had not changed by a single day.*

She couldn't take her eyes from the couple reflected in the mirror. An incredible couple, absurd, shocking. Yes, it was certainly Roland, the wonderful unharmed Roland of their love, Roland in her arms, her very flesh and soul. But *Roland just as he had been.*

But what about herself? What had happened to her? Who was that aging woman looking at her? That centenarian, that withered, desiccated mummy? Where had the peaches and cream, the bloom and softness, fled?

Only yesterday she had looked at herself in the mirror and found herself still passable, spared enough by the years to look several years younger than her age. But now, with her lover by her side, so completely unchanged, it was as though centuries had suddenly fallen upon her.

She started to weep again, sobbing like a little child. She didn't even try to understand why he had been spared the ravages of age. The secret was no longer of any importance. Only one thing remained—the horror of that image in the mirror. She turned from it with a shudder, looked for the door by which she had entered, was unable to find it, and moaning, her eyes dimmed with tears, she groped with her fingertips along the painted roses and lilies.

"I want to leave. I want to go away."

"No one can leave here," Roland said softly.

Chapter 28

Roland led Jeanne through the halls of the Citadel to the room that had been assigned her. They made their way through corridors as thronged and busy as streets, through a maze of stairways, a labyrinth of crossways, all gleaming white and reminiscent of the Casbah of Algiers that was so dear to Admiral Kemplin's heart. Overhead, all that could be seen was a crisscross of arches and ceilings painted in the gay blue of a summer sky, the color of happiness. A skillfully operated projector moved artificial clouds and flocks of lovely birds against this background.

Jeanne did not look at the ceilings; indeed, she scarcely saw anything at all. Nevertheless, she realized that she was moving through a dense crowd of men and women of all ages and races. There were many children as well, either entirely naked or adorned with some bit

of colored material, a flower, a jewel, a piece of lace.
These scraps of loveliness, however, were used only for
ornamentation and not as clothing to cover up their
bodies.

At the end of one passage, they came to a small ele-
vated place where a Provençal fountain played next to
an oleander bush. The round ceiling was painted to imitate a pale-blue sky. A tiny cloud revolved in the fashion of a watch hand to indicate the hours of the day.

As Roland pushed open a door, it started to sing like
a nightingale accompanied by the murmur of a spring.
He wanted to show Jeanne every detail of her new
home, but she looked about much in the manner of an
animal dying from a bullet wound, losing its blood drop
by drop, losing its warmth and finally its life. He made
her stretch out on a very soft bed, wanted to undress
her, but she shrank back in fright from his touch.

He said, "Tomorrow I'll explain everything. But now
you must sleep. You must recover from the shock
you've received. Don't be afraid. Everything is going to
be fine."

He was dressed in pale-green trousers, the trademark
of research scientists on 307, and a sort of collarless
jacket of the same color that opened and closed magnet-
ically and was abundantly supplied with pockets. He
drew from one of his pockets a syringe enclosed in a
plastic wrapping.

"It's to put you to sleep," he said. "Will you try it?"

She nodded "yes" but looked at him with questioning,
anguished eyes. He injected the serum into her thigh
through her trousers. Then he sat beside her on the bed,
took her hand, lifted it gently to his lips and kissed it.

She slowly closed her eyes and slept for thirty hours.

Chapter 29

"Master, I can't understand it. What is happening to me? For the past two days, I've been able to see in the dark. Not everything, only what is red. At night, everything red seems lit up."

Acharya, Bahanba's assistant, looked at his master with horrified eyes, like a frightened child turning to his father for reassurance.

"Look at these flowers."

He took all the red flowers from a bouquet on the table and held them out to Bahanba.

"Draw the curtains. Lower the blinds. Put out the lights, and I shall still see them. If you move them in the dark, I'll be able to tell you exactly where they are".

Bahanba had no need to engage in such an experiment. He was well aware of both the cause and the significance of this phenomenon of the night making all shades of red glow and change color from crimson to orange, from pale pink to scarlet.

For several years, he had devoted himself to the biological fight against cancer. He had experimented with chemical substances, the suspension of culture cells, then bacteria cultures and finally viruses. However, none of these experiments produced encouraging results.

Early in 1954, he inoculated a batch of white mice with a "plant" virus attenuated and irradiated by X rays. Two weeks later, he injected them with cells from a sarcoma, one of the most malignant forms of cancer. None of the mice developed a tumor. When a minute quantity of their blood was injected into other mice, these animals became resistant to cancer.

Thoroughly examining the blood of the immunized mice, Bahanba noticed nothing special about it until the day he saw its white cells develop a slightly blue stain when exposed to the international dye L3. As he had never succeeded in isolating the antibody this blood surely contained, or in finding "his" virus in it, he sent a sample of the "blue" blood to his friend Dr. Galdos of Harvard. Not daring to mention to Galdos the results he had obtained, Bahanba requested him to examine this blood under Harvard's superpowerful electronic microscope, which was the envy of all the laboratories in the world.

Two weeks later, he received a letter and photographs from Galdos, asking him where he had obtained "that," by which he meant minute particles in the shape of regular solid pyramids whose four sides were each equal triangles. Bahanba was not astonished at the way in which his own virus had changed its shape, for anything can be expected from a virus. He had not been able to detect the virus with the microscope at his disposal because, in passing from a geometric shape of six sides to one of four, the virus had reduced its dimensions in the proportion of a hundred to one. Thanking Galdos, he begged him to be patient and promised that he would be the first to know if his hopes should be confirmed.

These hopes were confirmed. Bahanba named his virus JL3, the letter J being the initial of his wife's first name and L3 the designation of the dye to which the infected blood had reacted. JL3 rendered mice resistant to any of the forms of cancer with which the learned scientist and his assistant inoculated them.

Bahanba was a genuine researcher, more avid for truth than for glory, and so sent a sealed phial of the JL3 virus to Professor Hamblain in Paris, to Adam Ramsay in London, to Galdos in the United States as well as to his habitual correspondents in Moscow, Munich and Peking. A note accompanying the phial stated that the results Shri Bahanba had obtained with the JL3 virus justified some hope for immunizing mice against sarcoma and other types of tumors. He specified in what manner and under what conditions he had used the JL3 and asked his correspondents to test it in their labs.

Acharya urged him to inform the medical world at large of his results. But, for fear of raising their hopes prematurely, Bahanba prudently decided to wait until his own results were confirmed by those of his correspondents. Then he would proceed to try out the JL3 on man. If the tests were positive, the world would finally be informed that the most terrible of diseases had been conquered.

But Bahanba did not wait to make his test on man.

In order to prevent any objection on Acharya's part, Bahanba sent him away for several months to an ashram in Benares. Immediately after Acharya's evening departure, Bahanba innoculated himself with the JL3 virus.

The night that followed the injection was very strange. He had worked late and felt age and fatigue weighing heavily on him. On returning home, he lingered in the gardens, enjoying the fragrant coolness of the night, listening to the thousand and one sounds made by the various insects in their obscure struggle for life. Passing the golden lantern burning perpetually before an empty altar, a symbol of one of the Hindu gods, he picked a budding rose and pressed it respectfully to his withered lips, breathing in the fresh fragrance of its petals. He carried it away with him, went directly to his room and placed it in a small vase in front of Siva.

And when he put out the light, he *saw* the rose in the dark.

He saw the red dot between Siva's eyebrows, the red powder spread over the statue's feet, the pale pink stripe of the curtains, a red tunic slung over an armchair like a flame, the interlacing of the red pattern of the carpet, the faces and hands of the figures of a rose tapestry on the wall and a whole mass of tiny red dots, lines and markings all about the room. He attributed this sudden sensitivity to red to the JL3 and wondered if it would last. The next morning, in the light of day, everything was normal. Before leaving for the laboratory, he took the rose of the night before and placed it on his left ear.

On arriving at the lab, he put the rose in the narrow flask he had been using the day before. Then, in order to take pleasure in the flower's beauty, he placed the flask on the table where he worked. It was a particularly beautiful rose, with an orange center not yet opened.

Bahanba wanted to find out if the nocturnal vision of the mice had been modified too. That evening, he put a misture of red and black seeds into the cage of several infected mice. The next morning, the black seeds remained but all the red ones had been eaten.

For him, this night had been similar to the preceding one. As he had walked in the gardens, all the flowers had seemed to be bathed in floods of light. The arborescent rhododendrons filled the dark with a display of every shade of red. They gave the illusion of hanging from the sky as they gently swayed in the breeze. It was a scene of breathtaking beauty that filled Bahanba with delight.

On the seventeenth day after he had inoculated himself with the virus, he grafted onto his left thigh a fragment of a human carcinoma in full evolution. After a short period of inflammation, the tumor took solid root. What started out as nothing more than a horrible little black spider on the brown skin of his thigh became enlarged and fleshy, like a hard plum. Shri Bahanba concluded from this that the virus that protected the mice was unable to protect man and that he himself was doomed to suffer a painful death from cancer. Even a prompt removal of the carcinoma would give him little chance of escaping a recurrence or a metastasis.

The day he decided to remove the tumor, it seemed to him that the carcinoma was less swollen and hard than the day before. He put off the operation to the next day, then to the day following. Within three weeks, the tumor had completely dried up and fallen off like a dead leaf.

Then Bahanba thought of the untold suffering that Brahma was going to allow him to spare his fellowmen through this discovery. He closed his eyes and thanked "That Which Is" in all his divine forms. He gave no credit to himself. The unexpected property of this root of a commonplace virus was due to the particular intensity and duration of irradiation to which he had exposed it. A split second more or less and the miracle would not have taken place. Chance alone had decided everything. But chance is one of the inumerable names of He Who Has Only One Name.

When Bahanba opened his eyes, his glance fell by chance on the shelf to which he had mechanically transferred the glass flask with the pink and orange rose of the first night. When had he carried the flask and the flower from the table to the shelf? That same day? The next day? He no longer remembered. It was at a moment when the little container had been in his way. That had been days and days ago. And since then, he had not looked in that direction. Or, if he had looked, preoccupied by his research, he had not *seen*. What he now saw was so astonishing that he thought he must be mistaken. He went over and picked up the flask to examine it more closely. There was no doubt about it, what had occured was unbelieveable and could only be due to a secondary effect of the JL3. The glass flask had retained a bit of the virus in an extremely diluted form.

Usually all the receptacles and instruments used for microbial cultures were dipped in an acid bath before being rinsed. This was done so that no living pathogenic germ would be carried away by the draining water. But Bahanba had used this flask at night, then placed it on the table before filling it with water the next day for the rose, so that it had undergone no acid bath. The JL3 had evidently been present in the flask and spread through the water he had put into it. There now remained no more than a few millimeters of that water in the bottom of the receptacle. But above . . .

Bahanba sat and pondered at length on the significance of what he had just seen. He succeed in controlling his emotions in order to permit his reason to function clearly, to admit a fact, no matter how incredible that fact appeared, and to draw his conclusions.

It was necessary to repeat the experiment scientifically. Bahanba asked his gardeners to bring him a living butterfly. They brought him a whole quivering bouquet of them. He set free all but one, which he enclosed in a glass casket along with a flower in whose calyx he had poured some honey diluted with water containing the JL3.

By the time Acharya returned from his religious retreat at Benares, Bahanba was sure of his facts and had taken the necessary precautions, which drew cries of protest and regret from Acharya. Bahanba insisted that this was the only course of action possible, that he could explain nothing, that he had to be believed on faith. Acharya's respect for his master was such that he lapsed into silence.

Bahanba had killed and incinerated the immunized mice and destroyed all the remaining JL3 in acid. He had written to his correspondents, asking them to destroy by fire or acid the contents of the phial he had sent them, as well as any animals on which the experiment had already been made, the virus having proven to be excessively dangerous.

Bahanba was assured by his correspondents that his

recommendation had been followed. No one seemed to have had the time to push the experiment far enough to get a clear idea of the real consequences of a JL3 innoculation. He was relieved to think that the virus he had artificially created now existed only in a small closet to which he alone had the key (and where he had locked away the flask and the glass casket) *and in his own bloodstream.*

And now, suddenly here was Acharya speaking of his "red" nights and unknowingly revealing that he too was a carrier of the JL3 virus. There was only one way he could have caught the virus, and that was so dangerous for the world that Bahnba could no longer keep the secret to himself. And yet, if he revealed what he knew, the danger would not be averted but in fact would become inevitable. Therefore, the secret must be shared solely with those men in the most highly responsible positions of power, the only ones who could take the necessary measures.

Bahanba immediately informed Achrya about the discovery and its consequences. At first, Acharya was completely bewildered and aghast, but he soon accepted the situation. They spent the night working and meditating, and the next morning Bahanba telephoned Pandit Nehru.

When Nehru had taken his seat facing Bahanba in the lab on the other side of the glass partition and had raised the telephone receiver to his ear, the scientist, speaking first in English and then in Sanskrit, had said, "This is what has happened. I have gained immortality. *And it is contagious!"*

Part 2

The Butterfly and the Rose

When Shri Bahanba had opened his eyes and looked toward the shelf at the flask into which he had placed the rose several weeks before, he saw that the rose was blooming as it had on the first day.

He took the flask in his hands to assure himself that it was the same rose, or rather to assure himself of the contrary, because he couldn't believe the reality of what he saw. A servant or a lab assistant had perhaps replaced the faded rose. But no, he recognized the orange center of the rose and the design of its petals. To test his hypothesis, he injected the JL3 into a thaumantis diores brown butterfly with blue markings whose lifespan was only thirty hours. He locked the water flask with its rose and the glass casket containing the butterfly in a closet to which he alone had the key.

Four weeks later, the butterfly and the rose were still alive and thriving. The butterfly had lived from twenty to thirty times the normal length of its life. Transposed to the human scale, that represented from one to two thousand years of existence.

Chapter 1

Thus, Shri Bahanba came to know that he was immortal. He had inoculated himself with the JL3 and, like the butterfly and the rose, he was—save for accident, poisoning, lack of water, air or food—going to live forever. He wanted to be certain of this and to know why. He went back to his mice.

Those he had inoculated with the JL3 virus were healthy, lively, gay, alert. He gave them injections of all the noxious germs in his laboratory, including the Plague. None of them died. None of them even became sick. Bahanba concluded that the JL3 had induced the manufacture of a universal antibody that rendered them immune to all illnesses. And the example of the butterfly and the rose showed that this antibody also protected living organisms against the most terrible of maladies—aging.

Death is an illogical absurdity in the realm of the living. It seems to have entered the scheme of things by accident or alien intervention. Nature has arranged its creation of life in such a way that a living organism, having reached the highest point in its development, should theoretically remain at that stage permanently. But it does not. Having reached its peak, it slowly, then faster and faster, begins to slip down the slope that leads to its destruction. Man begins to deteriorate at the age of eighteen. Just at the moment when they have barely left adolescence and imagine that they are on the threshold of life, man and woman have begun to pass their prime.

Without knowing it, they have started a losing battle against a malady from which nobody recovers.

The normal man should not be sick. The normal man should not get old. The fantastic constitution of his living body has received from the start the skill and the power to fight victoriously against all pathological attacks made upon it. But it seems as though in the course of time his defense mechanism has become mysteriously blocked. Vaccinations release this mechanism in part by making the body again capable of protecting itself over a limited time against certain microbes—for example, those of smallpox or tetanus. What Bahanba had discovered was the means of rendering man once more as invincible as he had been at the hour of his creation.

Chapter 2

Scientifically speaking, Bahanba would not be absolutely certain about the effect of the JL3 virus on human aging until he himself had exceeded the usual lifespan by an unwonted number of years. But he could not wait a hundred years to make a decision. The decision had already been formulated in his mind.

As a Hindu and a believer, Bahanba thought death to be a necessity, a door between two lives. It was only after having passed through an infinity of doors that the human soul became cleansed, purified, liberated and might then rejoin God. To suppress death was to close these doors, condemning embodied souls to remain forever as prisoners of matter, of illusions and of suffering. It meant servitude for all eternity.

Apart from any religious belief, what would happen if

the properties of the JL3 were divulged? The men in seats of power, reasoning that the danger of endowing everyone with immortality was too great, would restrict or prohibit the use of the vaccine—that is to say, they would reserve it for themselves. In this instance, a terrible inequality would arise in relation to life and death that would provoke the bloodiest revolts imaginable.

Or, on the other hand, in the name of equality and justice, all humanity would be inoculated over several years, and the density of the population would increase to such an extent that death would take its hideous revenge by way of famine, killing off old people and infants, indiscriminate poisoning from waste products and asphyxiation from pollution.

Bahanba knew all too well the effects of overpopulation and famine. In the streets of Calcutta, he had seen the trucks making their daily rounds to collect the bodies of children who had died from starvation. The JL3 virus could do nothing to alleviate that kind of horrible death. On the contrary, it could only render it universal. All the H-bombs in the world would wreak less havoc than immortality.

That is why, as soon as Bahanba was convinced that the JL3 had been destroyed by his correspondents as he had requested, his relief was overwhelming.

But now here was his assistant, Acharya, who had not received an inoculation of the vaccine but who had worked with Bahanba in the lab for three weeks, betraying the first symptom of infection by the virus. Either he had been infected with it by way of the mice before his departure for the religious retreat or, since his return, he had caught it from Bahanba himself. In both cases, the conclusion was the same: immortality was contagious.

When the virus had been injected into an organism, its presence was immediately revealed by the "red night" symptom. If it had been caught indirectly, however, it might circulate in the bloodstream for two months before attacking the system and generating the phenomenon of nocturnal vision. In both cases, the "infected" person only became contagious after the eleventh month.

Bahanba was not aware of all the ramifications. But he did know that every foreign scientist to whom he had sent the JL3 virus, as well as their families and personnel, might have been infected even if all the necessary precautions had been taken. Therefore, perhaps the groundwork for disaster was even now being laid. The virus would spread to all mankind if not to all forms of living matter. Bahanba envisioned a planet overwhelmed and submerged by a fantastic outburst of animal and vegetable life, with men, plants and animals overlapping and killing each other for space and food until death from starvation, asphyxia and total collapse.

It was imperative to effect immediately the removal of these sources of infection. Any person suspected of having caught the virus had to be withdrawn from circulation, with or without his consent, and exiled to a place totally isolated from the rest of the world. This could be done only with the support and assistance of the head of state of each country concerned and in the utmost secrecy. This was the reason for Nehru's "crusade" around the world. In the second plane that had followed Nehru's, Bahanba, secluded in an airtight compartment, met and talked with his correspondents by means of an interphone. He questioned them and, if necessary, revealed to them the properties of the JL3 virus, while Nehru explained the situation to each country's leader.

It took longer for the politicians to understand the consequences than it took the scientists, but they soon realized the enormity of the danger involved. The one leader easiest to convince was Eisenhower. He perhaps did not understand most of it very well, but being a general and President, he thought it was doubtless possible to use the JL3 virus for military purposes. He decided that it was better to restrict it to American territory than to let it go elsewhere and offered Islet 307 as a haven. He canceled the plans for an atomic explosion scheduled there and sent the Navy to guard the place and its installations.

Then the disappearances and kidnappings began. Roland Fournier had unwittingly given the signal for his own kidnapping when he told Jeanne on the telephone about his peculiar eye disturbances of the night before. When Bahanba left with his collaborators, his family and his servants, he carried with him the butterfly and the rose. The butterfly had by then lived more than seven hundred times the normal length of its life, which represented fifty thousand years of human life. And the rose was even older.

Part 3

Paradise

Bahanba was going to die.

He was the only one who knew it. Neither the children nor the adults, all of whom loved him, had the slightest suspicion that anything like that could possibly happen. Isolated from the rest of the world, the "real" world, life went serenely on, the absence of fear giving the days and nights an unaccustomed tranquillity. For those living in the other world, however, tomorrow was a day of both hope and fear: tomorrow, all pain and sorrow would cease; tomorrow, the score would have to be paid; tomorrow, perhaps the sun would shine; then again, tomorrow, somber winter might appear. But on the Island, the very notion of fear had disappeared. Tomorrow, no one would want for anything, no one would be a day older.

On the Island, tomorrow was a certainty.

Chapter 1

When Jeanne awakened, she found Roland waiting at the foot of her bed. Dressed in pale-green dungarees, he leaned over her with a smile. He was young and handsome, just as she had seen him on her arrival, untroubled, sure of himself. She looked at him with cool, unemotional eyes, as though he were a familiar object that she had set down on her bed table before falling off to sleep. Like an object one loves, but all the same, an object.

She felt extremely lucid, calm, controlled. She scrutinized Roland's face, searching for the look of the fifty-year-old man that in spite of everything he was, for a sign of what he had acquired during these past years and what he had lost. She saw that he had become experienced, reasonable, satisfied. Something in his eyes had died, though—anxiety and the impulse to escape it.

Jeanne clearly saw all that before she knew anything about the secret of the Island. She had vaguely guessed it but still had learned nothing specific. She felt herself ready to absorb and understand everything, to accept this world with all its surprises. "Did you drug me?" she asked.

"Yes," he replied. "I gave you an injection before you woke up, just to let you see and hear everything calmly. It will only last a day. After that, you'll be yourself again. And no one will interfere in your life unless you want them to. I give you my word."

He showed her how to use the telephone. It was simple: one only had to lift the receiver and give the name of the person to whom one wished to speak. The telephone operator here was electronic. It knew the name of each inhabitant of the Island, pronounced with no matter what accent, and found the person no matter where he was. It also took the order for breakfast, which was automatically wheeled into the room as it would be in a palatial hotel.

While Jeanne ate, Roland rapidly explained the basic facts about Bahanba's discovery. Then he went outside and waited for her by the fountain. While washing and dressing, she tried to think everything over. But her faculties of deduction and synthesis seemed to have been put to sleep. She was able to learn, register, know and to be objective. But she could neither contemplate and judge nor draw conclusions.

The bathtub noiselessly and quickly filled up from its bottom. The shower was equipped with horizontal spouts that sprayed Jeanne from the ankles to the shoulders. She hoped the icy water would wash away her aritificial tranquillity, but it didn't seem to help. She still felt protected from any judgment or feeling by an invisible carapace, as though she were walking in the rain surrounded by a transparent, waterproof cylinder. Unable to change her feelings, she accepted the situation.

In a closet, Jeanne found practical if not very elegant underclothes. At least they were less spartan than those given her by the Air Force, which she wore on her arrival. She also found several pairs of dungarees, like Roland's, but black and trimmed in bright blue. She put on a pair in her size and went to meet him.

Roland was sitting on the edge of the fountain. A well-fed red cat was asleep on his lap. Some exotic birds played in the bushes. The air smelled of the fresh odor of the country during a warm and lazy summer, and the murmur of the fountain gave off the peaceful sounds of vacation days. Roland told Jeanne that now everyone who saw her would know that she was a doctor. Each job or profession, manual or intellectual, was differentiated by the color or other detail of the clothing, as had once been the custom in villages during the distant past, when crafts and trades had flourished.

"It isn't obligatory; nothing is obligatory. It's simply a way to let others know one's profession without having to ask, and it helps to break down the wall between people."

She nodded her head, saying she understood. Roland was extremely pleasant. She gave him news of his wife, telling him how she had become a fat, rich, widowed drugstore owner. He smiled and said that he was happy for her. After a moment of silence, he added, "I had completely forgo 'n that she ever existed."

"And had you forgotten me?"

"You? Never."

It was the same matter-of-fact tone he would have used had she asked, "Did you forget your train tickets again?"

It was so spontaneous, so terrible, that in spite of the drug, she felt a sharp, icy sword pierce the screen of chemical opt: :m and run its sharp point into the center of her heart.

The pain didn't last. The wound closed up immediately, anestheti d by the drug. Jeanne became tranquilly indifferent once again. Roland said to her, "Come, let's take a tour of the place. You won't be able to see everything today, but I can at least show you the most important parts."

As they walked toward the center of the Island, Jeanne asked, "Do you live alone?"

She asked the question indifferently, simply for information.

He answered, "No one lives alone here for very long. Also, no one lives very long with the same partner. No human t 'ng can really envision spending all his life with the same man or the same woman when he knows that his life will last one or ten thousand years, maybe more. Here the wc d 'always' really means something. So, no one has enough courage to pronounce it. Couples come together and move apart wihout complications or bitterness, and they sometimes come together again. There are even some who stay together. The children know who their mother is and bear her name, but rarely know their father. Each man is the father of each child, and we love them all equally.

"Look," Roland said, "here is the future."

He had led Jeanne to a terrace overlooking a large circular garden from which arose sweet scents and laughter, joyful cries and the songs of children and birds. Leaning near her on a cement balustrade as delicate as lace, he pointed out to her with a proud sweep of his arm the new world.

Trees of all species spread their luxuriant branches toward the painted sky. The sky was as blue as the heavens in Rome, suffusing from some undetectable source a warm, comforting light on everything below. A few small white clouds slowly crossed the sky in changing forms. The sun was nowhere represented.

Climbing vines clung to the trees. Dense growths of shrubbery s. 'ead over the lawns. The lawns themselves were so thickly carpeted with flowers that one could hardly see the green grass beneath. The daisies, clover and great yellow dandelions created a mass of light. A crowd of naked children frolicked among the flowers which also formed a mantle over the trees and shrubs. Among the many species of plants unknown to her, Jeanne recognized rose trees in bloom, honeysuckles and white-caped jasmines all of whose leaves seemed to have been replaced by petals. A fantastic blend of the perfume of all the flowers of the world filled Jeanne's nostrils much like a carnal presence, a sustenance from paradise.

Rivulets flowed among the lawns, and brooks gushed at the roots of the trees or tumbled from their branches. Rabbits, squirrels, cats and guinea pigs played and pursued one another, climbed, leaped, disappeared into their burrows and holes. A fiery red fox rushed out from cover, attacked and carried off a rabbit. A charming adolescent girl with long slender arms knelt before a youth her own age, caressed the boy's sex with her soft hands and tongue, and when it stood erect, stretched out beside him on the bed of flowers, opened her body and guided his penis within. Younger children were playing games, rolling about on the daisies. A cat was eating a squirrel, swarms of multicolored birds flew from tree to tree as if sampling the different blooms, a heron pecked at a tiny frog.

"Here, nothing ever dies unless it's killed," Roland said.

A bell rang softly as though from far away in a country field, and a whole section of the sky turned white.

Some of the children raised their heads and shouted with joy on seeing, in place of the clouds, an old man's immense face appear. Waving their hands at him, they cried, "Grand-Ba! Grand-Ba!"

On hearing this name, the other children also looked up and shouted, then stretched out among the flowers to face the sky from where the old man looked down on them. He was extremely handsome, with a kind but weary air, and at the sound of his soft, low-pitched voice, the children became silent. One heard nothing now but the singing of the birds, the flow of the streams and the solemn voice coming from the sky. Jeanne was astonished to recognize words from the various languages that she spoke fluently, yet she understood nothing of what he said. The pair of adolescent lovers had not separated but now lay side by side to see and to listen.

"It's Bahanba," Roland said. "The children adore him. They call him Grand-Ba, which is a contraction of grandfather and of his name. He speaks to them in the language they have invented for themselves by mingling the various languages spoken by their parents. It is a living, shifting language in the process of creation, changing from day to day. I find it fascinating."

Jeanne looked very calmly at Roland, whose eyes were shining. The image of the old man faded away, and the small clouds started again on their slow circuit through the sky that once more was blue. Again the children started playing, running, falling, pursuing one another. The adolescent couple resumed their play, their bodies separating, then coming back together, changing position, with much sighing and laughter. A swarm of ocher, black and crimson butterflies took flight from the shrub they had coated. A long blue serpent, thick as a bottle, emerged from a white bush and undulated lazily across the daisy carpet. The younger children ran toward it, shouting with joy, lifted it and looped it into knots and curls. It coiled itself around them, making them stumble under its heavy weight. A boy of some ten years was trying to insert his small erect penis into a little girl who joined in laughingly, slipped from his grasp and finally beat him off with blows that sent him tumbling into a brook.

It was then that Jeanne noticed that in the garden there was no child younger than this girl or this boy. Roland told her that there were no others. The last birth to occur on the Island had taken place in May, 1962.

"It was a boy," he said. "I think it was my son, but I'm not sure."

They had reached a large round area that resembled both a marketplace and an airport lounge. Everywhere there were stalls of fruit tumbling out of their baskets with leaves and branches, and delicate displays of luxury items and necessities. Elevator doors opened between the stalls. Men and women of all ages quietly passed through them. But Jeanne noticed that whatever their race and the lined or unlined appearance of their faces, they shared a common freshness of complexion and a youthful skin tone.

"There are a lot of you."

"We live in a limited space. We're like passengers on a ship. It's big but can't get bigger. It's reached the limit of the number it can hold. That's why we stopped having children ten years ago. We were forced to stop population growth completely. So, we added birth-control medication to the food made each day. All the women absorb it without having to think about it and remain sterile."

Passing in front of the stalls, the adults and children took handfuls of grapes and cherries, stockings, cigarettes. They didn't pay. There were no shop keepers to look after the merchandise.

"You haven't answered my question," Jeanne said.

"What question?"

"Do you live alone?"

He stopped and faced her. The crowd milled around them like crowds in a subway station but in a setting like that of a provincial operetta.

"I've been living alone ever since I knew you were coming. I separated from Lony. I had been living with her for several months."

"You separated from her because of me?"

"It's closer to the truth to say we left each other."

"You made that sacrifice?"

He smiled and replied, "There was no sacrifice involved. She'll be as happy with someone else as with me."

"And you too?"

He ceased smiling and, after a short silence, answered, "What matters is that you be happy."

"How old is she?"

"Lony?"

"Yes."

"Oh well, age here, you know. . . ."

"What age does she look?"

He slipped a hand under her arm and took her calmly toward an elevator. He tried to appear casual, as though nothing of what they were discussing had any importance.

"She was fourteen or fifteen when she arrived with her parents from the United States. She was stabilized at eighteen."

"Stablized?"

"That's the word we use. The JL3 lets everything that lives grow to its prime and then keeps it from going downhill. And this prime, whether in vegetables or animals, is always the age of love. For the plants it's the flower. In the spring, in Normandy, an apple tree demonstrates its pleasure in lovemaking by its 100,000 flowers. How can we think that plants have no feeling when they express in such an incredibly luxurious fashion the most marvelous joy the world has to offer?"

He suddenly became aware that what he was saying was perhaps agonizingly painful for the woman he was leading through the crowds of gay, insouciant people. She had once known with him this blooming joy, so carnal, so cosmic, that came from the beginning of life's creation itself and streaked like a shooting star toward the future. And while he was speaking to her, she must be telling herself that she would never again know such bliss. And then he realized that from the moment he had left her, he himself had never again experienced that passionate delight. Lony and the others had nothing to do with fire and passion and love. They offered only the game itself and rapid pleasure, transient as a train passing over the rails, shaking them but leaving no trace.

Jeanne started to speak, but Roland didn't want to give her time to think about anything. Silencing her with a gesture, he quickly continued in a slightly professorial tone, like a teacher dodging a student's embarrassing question.

"In order that the fruit be born, the flower must fade, die and disappear. The fruit, the seed, is already in a state of deterioration, the decline of one life giving birth to another. Germination is not only birth, it is death. That was the real meaning of the myth of Adam and Eve—*the apple is decay*. Adam and Eve should have remained flowers. That is no longer possible, even here, for men or for animals But it has become possible for the entire vegetable kingdom. The JL3 does not allow the flower to fade and die. It stops its transformation just before the first second when it would begin to grow old. All the fruit that you see has been sent here by the world outside. We can't grow any here. In our paradise, no fruit can come into existence. But our flowers are immortal."

Chapter 2

Bahanba had not thought of this danger. He saw it clearly and understood its ramifications only after he had lived on the Island and observed the way in which the plants and animals existed. If the JL3 virus had been spread throughout the world, animals would have multiplied, but certain plants of the vegetable kingdom would have disappeared because they couldn't reproduce themselves by seed. And man would have found himself suddenly deprived of the essential ingredients of his diet: no more fruit, or vegetables, or rice or corn. Not a grain of wheat would have been left on earth.

In the animal kingdom, the flower is the couple. One half of the couple is the young female in full bloom. But the impregnated female can produce fruit and separate from it without that act leading to her decline and death. Therefore, the JL3 virus did not prevent her from becoming a mother.

In the insect kingdom, it is neither the caterpillar nor the pupa nor the larva nor the chrysalis that the JL3 immortalized, because all those forms are only transitory preparations for the perfect form, the form that has wings and is ready for love—the dragonfly or the butterfly. The male butterflies die after having impregnated the females, and the females die after having given birth.

On the Island, the butterflies never died from natural causes. Bahanba's butterfly was still alive at the age of eighteen. On the human scale, that meant a life-span of four hundred thousand years!

Chapter 3

Roland and Jeanne had arrived in front of an elevator whose doors slid open to let out a group of passengers. Two men dressed in blue nodded in a friendly fashion to Roland. He and Jeanne entered the elevator with another group.

"First," said Roland.

"Fourth," said an American woman.

A Chinese man uttered a word that Jeanne didn't understand but which the automatic elevator apparently did. It began to descend noiselessly.

Roland continued to lecture Jeanne.

"A woman reaches the height of her physical perfection at about eighteen years, a man slightly later. Here, they reach that summit without having suffered any illnesses. And they never go downhill after that. All the children who have come to the Island or have been born here will remain at the age of eighteen forever. Unfortunately, those of us who have already passed it. . . ."

He said "we" kindly as though he put himself in the same age group as Jeanne, he so physically superb and she . . . Because of the drug, she felt neither disturbed nor unhappy. Jeanne was like the broken and lacerated victim of a traffic accident who, having awakened after being mended by the surgeons, knows that the pain is there inside her, hidden somewhere underneath the morphine, and that the moment will come when it will make itself felt.

"We can't regain our youth. Bahanba isn't Mephistopheles. We remain as we were when we arrived on the Island. Only the children change and grow until they reach the age of perfection."

The elevator had slowly descended. Nothing was of any urgency on the Island. Everyone had *all* the time in the world.

The elevator had stopped, its doors opened and Jeanne asked, "That means that—"

"That what?"

"That Lony will be eithteen eternally?"

"Yes," Roland said.

Chapter 4

Han and Annoa came out from behind a mass of bushes covered with flowers. They were extremely beautiful as they walked hand in hand toward the other youngsters. They were still children, but at the same time they were already a man and a woman in the innocence and glory of their life.

They trod lightly, their bare feet buried in the grass and daisies. Han was fifteen, the son of an American atomic physicist of Irish origin and a woman born of Polish immigrant parents. He was tall and slim, with blue eyes and blond hair cascading to his shoulders. His newly sprouting, sand-couored pubic hair was very pale against his suntanned skin.

Annoa was fourteen, the daughter of an Indian mother and a Chinese father. She was fragile and sweet, with immense, slanted black eyes, hips and breasts just beginning to bud, long, slim hands and smooth, coal-black hair. They had not parted for a moment since their first day and night together at the start of Bahanba's fast, seven days earlier.

Bahanba had decided to begin the year with a total fast of seven days' duration, as an experiment in purification and to understand death more clearly. He had told only his favorite doctor how far he meant to go. He had lain down to rest for his fast among the children playing on the thick grass of the round garden. He had stretched out in the center of a lawn bordered by a brook and rosemary bushes, wearing his white robe, with his white hair spread in the grass around his lined, peaceful, dark face. He had closed his eyes when he lay down, after telling the children that he was going to fast, and he did not open them again for seven days. His arms were stretched lengthwise alongside his body, his hands opened toward the earth so that his palms rested against the grass. The children continued to play around him, but even the youngest tried to smother their laughter and moderate their cries and gestures, so as not to unduly disturb his tranquillity.

Chapter 5

The children of the Island were free. They ate what and when they wished and slept where they desired, with rooms always available either next to their mother or away from her. Sometimes they preferred to spend their nights in the garden.

A child learned as the spirit moved him, depending on his desire and inclination. There were courses on every possible subject, from reading and writing to the most advanced studies. Also, the old crafts and trades, all that man had made with his hands for hundreds of thousands of years, were taught. At twenty, some young people revealed their talents or genius, while others still didn't know how to read, write or add. They had plenty of time. They were all happy. One never heard a child cry.

Chapter 6

Bahanba had begun his fast on the morning of January 9, the second Sunday of the year. He had spent the preceding night in meditation before coming down among the children to remain for the seven days. The children decided to fast along with him. They told him this, laughing, leaping and shouting when he arrived in the garden. Many fasted until the middle of the day; some of the older ones were able to last until evening; still others continued through the second day; Han and Annoa, however, fasted for three full days.

When night fell on the first day, many children slept in the garden with Grand-Ba. A boy named Den had lit a fire on the small gravel beach near the brook. Kneeling in its light, he hummed a tune in rhythm with the small, dancing flames. He had made himself an instrument that resembled a banjo with a warm tone. Den was English.

He knew who his father was because his mother had been pregnant when his parents had arrived on the Island. Since that time, they had amicably separated, as had most of the other families. Very early, Den had had an irresistible desire to leave the Island. He couldn't stand being enclosed and wanted to sail away and discover what was outside. But at the other end of the seas, there was no unknown mystery, only the pitiless world of men prey to that terrible thing the adults called death. The world could not be delivered from its malediction, and its sufferings would become more terrible still if one arrived there, contaminated, from the Island. So, Den consoled himself by singing. He sang that the day would come when he would leave the Island for distant lands across wide seas.

In September, 1971, when he learned of the existence of Project Gilead, he seized on it as just what he wanted, the true departure, the real ship. He asked to work with the adults and was admitted to their group. Although he was only fourteen, he was quite advanced in physics and mathematics and very adroit in mechanics and electronics. He also knew how to make a piece of steel furniture and how to construct a lock and key or a magnetic combination for it.

On this January evening, as he was humming, a group slowly formed around him. Some listened, others sang along with Den. When Han came to sit down next to Den, he sang out the name of Grand-Ba.

Annoa came and sat next to Han.

Han and Den resembled each other. They were both blond and slim, but Han was golden and Den rather pale. Han was a dreamer and Den practical, but they had the same passionate nostalgia for voyages. Han often jumped into an enclosed bark, raced like a madman around the Island, brushed against the red buoys and one day almost went beyond them. Driven back by the threats proffered over the Admiral's loudspeakers, he had returned to the confines of the Island, consumed by a kind of desperation. But daily pleasures, work and games, quickly chased away his yearnings.

Han and Annoa had known each other as do all children in a small village. They had seen each other every day but had never truly looked at one another. As Annoa bent down to sit next to Han, he glimpsed, in the light of the fire, the small vertical mouth at the bottom of her belly and the tips of her tiny round breasts, and his artless sex became erect. She saw it, smiled, gave it a glancing caress as though it were a small kitten, then place her arm around Han, leaned her head on his shoulder and began to sing along with him. The voices stopped, the children lay down and slept. Grand-Ba had not moved since morning. Annoa also stopped singing and closed her eyes. Han continued to sing, but it was now a hymn of love in Annoa's ear to show the joy he felt when she leaned her head on his shoulder.

Then he ceased to sing because he saw that she was beautiful. He had been born on the island in its first days, and since then no one had ever said to him "This is beautiful" or "That is ugly." And when he watched Annoa sleep, her face lit by the fire, he was stunned by her beauty and felt impelled to tell her so. He lay down next to her and, while she slept, whispered in her ear, "How beautiful you are!" He was certain that she heard his words in her dreams.

Dawn began to break, rosy and then golden. The children still slept, stretched out on the grass as though they had fallen from the sky. Then, as they began to move, the animals began to leave their burrows and holes in the trunks of the trees. A lark flew straight upward, singing, toward what it believed to be the limitless blue sky, hit the ceiling, fell down, began to fly up once more and continued to do this without losing courage. Annoa rose and left for several minutes, returning with her arms full of fruit, fresh rolls, newly baked bread. She held out a peach to Han, who sat up rubbing his eyes. He took it and opened his mouth to take a bite, then stopped and asked, "Grand-Ba?"

They looked at Bahanba, who had not moved. His robe and his white hair billowed around him still. Han put the peach down on the grass.

"I'm going to continue to fast," he said. "Have you eaten?"

She shook her head from side to side, kneeling in front of him. Again, he was struck by her beauty and said, "How beautiful you are!"

Laughing, he pushed her back onto the grass. She got up and fled. He chased after her, abandoning the food to the others, animals and children alike, who quickly devoured it.

Annoa reached the brook and jumped in, followed by Han. They played in the water like two baby seals, then got out and stood facing one another, the water streaming from their hair and over their skin.

Slim and slight, she reached as high as his chin. He picked her up and carried her far from the others, laid her down among the lavender and began to kiss her all over. He had often lain with girls but had never kissed them and so was awkward about it. She took his head between her hands and brought his lips properly against hers. Their lips did not open at first but lay against each other like pink roses. Hunger made them slightly lightheaded. They held each other firmly and were filled with unadulterated happiness.

When he entered her, their emotion was so extraordinary that together they uttered a long deep sigh of deliverance, as though they were on the threshold of life or of death.

Han had already made love to girls and Annoa to boys, but only as a friendly game. This time, everything was new for them and therefore incredible. And each time they made love again, that day or in the days that followed, they experienced the same astonishment, the same sense of discovery as they had the first time.

They stayed in the garden the entire day, seeing only each other. They wordlessly walked hand in hand, laughing out loud with happiness. They sat down, he pushed her back in a reclining position, knelt to see her better and always murmured the same words over and over again: "How beautiful you are!" She closed her eyes to let the words enter her head and warm the interior of her body. He caressed her everywhere with his fingertips, the palms of his hands, his forehead, his lips. He was overtaken by a frenzy of joy and plunged his face into her breasts, her belly, her sex, moaning with pleasure as she laughed happily and clasped him against her without opening her eyes. She moved along with him, tenderly, softly. Every bit of her body was offered to him, open to receive him, absolutely relaxed, with no obstacles between them. It was not happiness, it was not joy, it was something that could not have a name in life because it was greater than life.

Finally, Annoa slept the deep sleep of the beloved, calm and peaceful like a quiet sea. Han fell asleep beside her. They slept all night entwined in a close embrace.

The following day, they fasted again and forgot their hunger in the great love feast they shared with each other. At the end of that day, Annoa went to get some food and they ate it while sitting on the branch of a linden tree surrounded by the perfume of its flowers. It was the end of their voyage with Bahanba. Han and Annoa had fasted longer than any of the other children, until the end of the third day. And since the birth-control medication was given to girls diluted in the food, Annoa, because she had fasted, was pregnant.

Chapter 7

On the fifth day, the children began to worry. Bahanba had still not moved, and there were no signs of his breathing. The doctor who placed a stethoscope on his thin chest heard nothing for several seconds. Then there was a slow and powerful heartbeat. The heart beat eleven times to the minute, which is what Bahanba had predicted before beginning his fast. The doctor reassured the children. He returned the next day to find the heart beating five times, and on the seventh day, the heart beat only three times to the minute. That evening, the doctor listened for two minutes before hearing the heart beat once. He then placed his hands over Bahanba's eyes and pressed down, as Bahanba had ordered him to do. Bahanba's chest heaved, and the doctor lifted his hand. Bahanba opened his eyes and smiled. The children waited silently while the doctor held out a sip of water in a bowl to the old man. He drank for the first time in seven days. He had gone very far indeed into the knowledge of his own body and the meaning of death. He now knew what he had wanted to discover. He sat up and called the children to him with a wave of his long, thin hand. They ran to him with explosions of joyous laughter, the birds and butterflies flew wildly in the air and the red fox began to chase his tail around a tree.

Chapter 8

The car waiting for Samuel Frend at Washington National Airport conducted him to the White House, where he had a private meeting with President Johnson lasting for two hours. By the end of the conversation, he knew that he had lost his liberty, his identity and his family. He had accepted a mission that was going to take the rest of his life and perhaps end it.

President Johnson possessed a complete dossier on Frend. The agent's intelligence and impartiality, his obstinance in following up on the ramifications of Mr. Smith's Dallas appearance and, the determining element, his scientific knowledge, had all contributed to the President's decision. Frend would be told of the existence of the Island and, in a general way, of the hope and mortal danger it represented for humanity, but the exact nature of that danger and hope would not be disclosed. President Johnson could not take a chance on Frend's endurance under torture by any of the world's secret services. The only way to keep him from revealing the secret was to leave him in ignorance of it. But in order to persuade Frend to accept the fact that he would .·ever see his wife and children again, that he would disappear as Samuel Frend and perhaps, at the end of his work, that he would to die a violent death, it was necessary that the President give him proof of the fantastic importance of his mission. And this proof was provided over the telephone by the heads of state of France, Great Britain, the U.S.S.R. and China, who assured

124

him that the international anguish over this problem was such that it went beyond any political boundaries. Frend's mission had been planned by all the great powers together, and it was they who would one day decide again the fate of the man who had been chosen to execute this plan. And not only his fate, but that of the Island itself.

About two years after Frend's visit to the White House, the body of a thin, bearded man was found in Central Park. He had died from three knife wounds, two in the stomach and one in the heart. There were no papers or money on him, as he had obviously been robbed. But his fingerprints, after having passed through innumerable police and secret-service checks, ended by reaching the Pentagon, where they were identified as belonging to Samuel Frend. His family was asked to view his remains, but the body by this time was in such a state of decomposition that all they showed his wife was an old silver cigarette lighter that had been found beside the corpse. She broke into tears when recognized it as one she had given him when they had been living in Paris.

Samuel Frend was declared dead. Actually, under the alias Samuel Bas, he had been made a colonel and was continuing to prepare for his mission. At the Army's atomic-research center in New Mexico, he participated for two years in the fabrications of A-and H-bombs. He had spent the two preceding years perfecting his knowledge of nuclear physics with the team of an eminent Italian physicist, who would have been astonished if he had known what activity was being prepared by his American student, whom he knew as a melancholy, relaxed, slightly nearsighted milk drinker.

In November, 1966, Frend-Bas—now promoted to the rank of general—left the center in New Mexico and became an engineering trainee at New Electronics, a firm making miniature radio receivers and amplifiers for

N.A.S.A. At the end of 1966, he took up his Army post again and was put at the head of a department created especially for him. It was given the code name of "Apple Two," which meant absolutely nothing. On a marshy plain not far from Houston, Texas, he and his associates occupied a group of workshops and offices surrounded by an electrified fence guarded by armed sentries and savage police dogs.

The care that Frend and his associates took to hide the fact that they were working for N.A.S.A. convinced the secret agents swarming around Apple Two that General Bas must be working on a new military satellite. And indeed, in the air-conditioned and sterilized central hangar, hooded technicians were constructing a machine that could be mistaken for a satellite.

Under cover of his mock activity, General Bas was able to continue safely with the construction of the machine he really needed. He ordered the different parts from sub-contractors, each of whom knew only about the piece of machinery he personally was making, which could perfectly well have served as a component of a satellite, military or not. The technicians working at Apple Two received these pieces of equipment and assembled them in several separate workshops. They also believed that they were constructing some sort of official satellite.

In July, 1970, the different elements of the project were finished and lay separate but ready in the various workshops of Apple Two site. Frend then made a lightning voyage around the world to see Mao, Brezhnev and Nixon. He gave each of them a white case the size of a small package of cookies and another, smaller case. The latter was an atomic chronometer that varied only several tenths of a second per year. The three chronometers were synchronized with each other and with the time belt of Islet 307.

Frend returned to Apple Two and, alone in his bullet-proof office and workshop, added the final touches to his machine. When completed, it resembled a large blue suitcase made of fiberglass.

Two months later, Frend was in France, at the head of a technical mission charged with the mounting and delivery of certain essential pieces fabricated for the French Atomic Center by General Electric. In June, 1971, when the Island requested supplementary material and personnel for its own atomic center, Frend, as Samuel Bas and with the title of atomic engineer, was in the group of three technicians who landed there. The two others were a Chinaman and a Frenchman. They brought with them two barges full of material and luggage, among them the blue valise of Apple Two.

Chapter 9

Roland and Jeanne continued their tour through the Citadel.

"You know, we have the time, if ever anyone did, and we're dispassionate about things. That's why we plan on trying out everything. Right now, we're making the Island into a laboratory for the world, and we will be able to remember our experiments for centuries. When we discover something really worthwhile, we'll give it to the rest of the world. For instance, we're trying out almost total liberty. Some things are forbidden in order to safeguard individuals, the Island and the world, but nothing is obligatory, not work, or timetables or attendance anywhere. No one is forced to do anything."

After visiting the gardens, Roland led Jeanne into the

depths of the Island, toward the workshops and factories. They rarely took elevators, walking down short flights of staircases that were often joined by gently sloping ramps. The population of the Island walked as though they knew where they were going and why, but without haste or urgency, since they had all the time for anything they could want to do.

Flowering plants climbed the walls, which contained windows with green shutters. Trees and fountains decorated the squares. Sometimes, a "street" opened out onto a country landscape or a mountain, and it was only upon close inspection that Jeanne could discern that it was painted. A light cool breeze blew everywhere. The atmosphere was gay and sunlit.

As Jeanne and Roland descended into the interior of the Island, they met fewer children and passersby. They found some youngsters asleep in a room that seemed to have a thousand pumps. Roland told her that each time he passed through this installation, he came upon several children so deeply asleep that they seemed more mineral than human. He thought it might be the hum of the motors and the water that attracted them, and put them to sleep. Jeanne herself wanted to lie down beside them.

These pumps transformed seawater into freshwater and then circulated it through the Island. Once the water was used, it was brought to a softening and purifying plant, where it was mixed with new water and then sent back through the system. Each pump was directed by a computer.

"This is our heart," said Roland, "the steady, unfaltering heart of the Island. We finished the installation several months ago. Obviously, we didn't construct it ourselves. We conceived and designed the plans and sent them out by telegraph. In the fleet that circles the Island, there's a ship especially equipped to receive any plans we might make. Our specifications are handed over to whichever company can produce the best results in the shortest length of time. We have priority over everything, even over war materials. The components are delivered to us in separate parts and we assemble them ourselves. Everyone works on it. Each person, although independent, feels an obligation to the others, simply because he's *not* forced to do anything."

Jeanne's head had begun to spin with all she was learning.

"What's so astonishing is that it works," she said.

"We have enough technicians and skilled workers to direct our work. Some of the best hands and the best minds of our time are here."

They left the children still sleeping and went farther down to visit the atomic center, silent and boiling hot, bathed in a red light, where men dressed and masked in yellow moved about noiselessly. The atomic pile was a revolutionary model that left no residue. It was situated at the deepest point inside the Island, directly above the old 1955 bomb that, because of President Eisenhower's decision, had not been exploded. Rather than move it, they had simply defused it, and its fissionable metal constituted an eventual reserve for the station.

Chapter 10

Bahanba opened the door of a closet and took out the glass case in which the butterfly of Bombay rested. The ancient insect was lying on a cotton bed. Its sublime wings, made to exist for only a day, were broken, fallen into dust. It tried to move them from time to time, but instead of flying, the butterfly simply trembled.

Of its frail broken legs, only the stumps remained, and they moved vaguely on the sides of its chest. Its spiral-shaped proboscis, which had once unfolded to hunt for nectar deep inside flowers, had shrunk close to its head. But it had learned over the years to make use of what remained. Bahanba placed a sliver of glass before it. He had let fall on the glass a drop of water filled with honey and vitamins. He lifted the sliver carefully until the insect's head brushed the liquid. The rudiments of its wings quivered and the drop of water was sniffed up.

Over the years, this marvelous insect had been reduced to its essential parts. It was now only a simple pouch enclosing its insides and their nerve endings. All the external attributes that had given it individuality and beauty had disappeared. If it had been a lizard, the JL3 would have allowed it to grow its tail again ten thousand times because that kind of regeneration is in the nature of the lizard. But it is not in the nature of the butterfly to grow its lost wings again.

It is, however, in the butterfly's nature to lay eggs if it is a female. This one was a female and had already been impregnated when Bahanba's gardeners in Bombay had captured it for him. For seventeen years now it had lain eggs hour by hour, without stop.

Affectionately, Bahanba had given it a name—Bahi. He had patiently destroyed by acid and fire the millions of eggs that Bahi had laid over the years. If he had permitted them to hatch, millions of caterpillars would have become millions of immortal butterflies that would in turn have laid millions of eggs. The caterpillars of the fifth generation would have covered the entire surface of the earth at a thickness of about three feet.

But then those crawling creatures would have been dead of hunger well before that, having devoured everything.

Chapter 11

Roland and Jeanne were eating lunch on a beach. Most of the upper section of the Island was occupied by a saltwater swimming pool surrounded by a make-believe seaside. Tiny waves flowed onto white sand. As in the streets and gardens, there were many children, men and women in bathing suits or in the nude. The breeze was warm, and real palm trees gave the artificial beach a background reminiscent of California.

"The scenery is changed each year. No one could stand the idea of going to the same beach for ten thousand years," Roland explained.

"It's simply not possible," Jeanne said, astonished by the extravagant possibilities of this future. "I can't believe you could really face the idea of living ten thousand years here without budging, without leaving, shut up like this. Not even for a thousand years. Not even for a hundred! How long have you been here?"

"Seventeen years. But it seems as if I just arrived last week. Everything is so exciting."

Jeanne looked at him gravely and said softly, "Last week? I've been looking for you for a century."

"I'm sorry, my dear," he said.

Roland leaned toward her and took her hand in his. She drew it away slowly, looking sadly at it. Her hand, compared to his, was so old. Did he remember how warm and soft this hand of hers had been, how well it had known how to caress his sex and bring it back to life after its exquisite fatigue due to hours of lovemaking? But this hand was no longer of those years, of that place. There was nothing in common, nothing, between the Jeanne of the rue du Vaugirard and the Jeanne of the Island today.

"I must have been mad. What was I running after? Our youth? Well, now I've caught it."

She was lucid now, no longer melancholy. The drug had simply rendered her indifferent. Roland shrugged.

"Our youth? What does that mean? What importance is there in being thirty or fifty in the face of the thousands of years of life lying before us? We're together at the beginning of everything, as if we are living our first days together."

Smiling, he took her hand again. She looked at it as though it were an alien object. He was right. What did twenty years more or less mean when now there was time without end? This dried-up hand between his smooth ones for ten thousand years?

The bell tolled softly, indicating noontime. It could be heard everywhere on the Island, giving the hour all through the day without emphasis, familiar, charming, slightly melancholy when the light became dark blue it was time to sleep.

"Only noon. I've made you walk a lot this morning. Are you exhausted?"

"No, I'm all right. Is there any way of avoiding it?"

"Avoiding what?"

"Do people like me who arrive on the Island without having the virus necessarily catch it?"

"Most of them. There are exceptions. In the Middle Ages, when the Plague was rampant, there were some people who never fell sick. The JL3 is more contagious than the Plague, but there are a few who do resist it. We've already seen it happen in two cases."

"Then there are two people here who are growing old? Like ordinary people?"

"No. It seems that if contamination hasn't taken place

after two months, it means that the organism is immunized against catching the virus in the usual way. The two people who were immune asked for an injection at the end of that time. We took blood from one of us who had the same blood type and injected it into a vein. After several hours, the JL3 virus began to work."

He had continued to hold Jeanne's fragile hand in his. Because of the drug, she was no longer aware of it, and he didn't know what to do with it. He raised it to his lips, gave it a light kiss and placed it on the table.

"But if one doesn't wish to be given the injection, does one have to have it?"

"No one is forced to do anything," he replied.

Chapter 12

Khrushchev was the first to realize that, despite all the precautions taken, eventually the JL3 virus would probably escape from the Island and contaminate the world. And life, delivered from the restraint of death, would begin to multiply, to blossom, to explode, to overrun itself. In spite of the cataclysms that would follow, despite death's brutal revenge by way of wars, famines and massacres, life would not cease after each disaster but would begin again, invading everything everywhere and producing havoc and devastation. Life without death would render life impossible. What could be done? How could an impenetrable wall be erected to stop this menace?

Only one mosquito would be enough to set the earth on fire. A mosquito might sting an inhabitant of the Island and draw out some blood containing the virus. Then a fish might eat the mosquito and be eaten by another fish, and the eggs of the fish be eaten by hundreds of fish and their eggs and themselves be eaten by ten thousand fish and birds of the sea, with the birds dropping their excrement in the oceans and on land. Eventually, of course, the chain would reach man.

Khrushchev, who had received his phial of JL3 from a leading Russian scientist, thought over what could be done to avoid such a fate. That was in 1955, at a time when some of the more imaginative science-fiction writers had predicted the first expedition of man toward the moon in the year 2050 or even much later.

When Nehru had visited Moscow, several weeks earlier, he had confided the secret of the JL3 only to Khrushchev. Although Malenkov had resigned, Khrushchev did not yet have complete control of the reins of power. But Nehru, who knew how to judge men, thought he would soon be the man to make the decisions in the Soviet Union and so spoke to him.

At that time, in Russia as in America, vague studies had been made about the possibility of navigation outside the terrestrial atmosphere. But aside from a few fanatic specialists, no one was much interested in them. And in Russia, they had more need for trucks, wheat, butter, shoes and arms than for trips to the moon.

Khrushchev called a meeting of the Politburo to hear the specialists concerned with space projects, including technicians of all kinds, astrophysicists, economists and generals. He declared that for reasons that could not be made public, that he could not reveal even to them, reasons that placed the Soviet motherland before an alternative of life or death, it was urgent to prepare for interplanetary voyages.

It was as though he had thrown a dog into a hen house. The specialists of the Cosmos project were elated, while the others protested. Such disputes would have been unthinkable during Stalin's lifetime.

Khrushchev pounded his fists on the table, raised his voice and declared that the solar system would belong to those who were the first to land on the moon and that the United States was ready!

This wasn't true and he knew it. But his declaration justified his request to ask that project Cosmos be given top priority status.

On October 4, 1957, the astonished world learned that the first Sputnik was revolving around the earth.

By November, 1964, Khrushchev had fallen from power, but he had passed on the secret to Brezhnev. However, Khrushchev did not tell his successor that in Paris, on May 15, 1960, a phial of the JL3 virus had been stolen from him.

Chapter 13

Roland continued to proselytize Jeanne.

"We have all the time in the world. And we'll always have our memories. Men have already tried all possible ways of living together in society—from the clan and the horde as nomads up to consumer capitalism and communism. Whatever the system adopted, there are always those who profit from it and others who don't accept it. Most of the time, it ends in bloody revolt. The system that is destroyed is replaced by its antithesis, which succumbs in turn to another system of government. Experiences and experiments accumulate to no purpose since they are soon forgotten. Each generation is willing to accept the wealth and the knowledge acquired by the preceding generation, but not its wisdom. A child accepts, even demands that you feed it, but when you tell it that fire burns, it does not believe you until it has put its finger in the flame. Each generation must undergo its trial by fire, each generation must get burnt. But what is new here on the Island is that we have no generations. Our children will not have children, as there isn't any room for them. They will grow up and join us and together we're going to try out different systems during centuries, during thousands of years, without calling everything into question all the time, because we, we will remember!"

Chapter 14

A satellite was put into orbit that brought it over the Island once a day. It had been launched at Cape Canaveral by the United States military. It belonged to the category of clandestine satellites, stationary or mobile, which form a belt around the earth, scrutinizing it night and day, making an inventory of its mountains, deserts, rockets, factories, leaves and specks of dust. The quantity of information those satellites send to the general staffs of the two blocs is so vast that they would need a thousand years to read, interpret and utilize it all. They give so much information that the result is the same as if they gave none. Of course, the general staffs were ignorant of the reason why this particular satellite was fixed above the North Pacific. They had received the order to launch it and had watched it leave, but they knew nothing more about it.

The satellite served to assure communications between the Island and the great powers. It also transmitted radio and TV programs from the major nations to the inhabitants of the Island. The Island was materially self-sufficient, but it had to be prevented from becoming limited in its scope and understanding. The men living there were rather exceptional in that they were going to live longer than succeeding generations of ordinary men. It was imperative that they always remember that, aside from this physical longevity, they too were ordinary men.

The fact that this was not true did not diminish the importance of preventing the Island from becoming the refuge of a superhumanity totally separated from an irrational and mortal humanity. The privileged people on the Island had to continue to feel a solidarity with the transitory beings who trampled each other underfoot, made mistakes, fought and died each day on television. That is why a permanent wavelength current was set up between the satellite and the Island and a television antenna was erected on the rock.

The reason the word "ordinary" was difficult to apply to the Island's inhabitants is easy to understand. If we knew that we would have all the time possible, that death would only come in ten or one hundred thousand years or perhaps never, would we remain ordinary? If we knew that we would have all the time possible to recover from sadness or pain for forgetfulness, all the time possible to know *everything* and to love a thousand times, each time the length of a life, without ever growing old, would we still be possessed by our mortal frailties? The heads of state in on the secret tried to persuade themselves that it was possible to remain "ordinary" under those circumstances, if the outside world could really be *seen*.

Those world leaders numbered only four by now. Adenauer had believed that he had plenty of time to pass on the secret to the new German Chancellor, but he did not and so he took the secret with him to the grave. And the five chiefs who remained had decided that it was just as well to leave Germany ignorant of the affair. De Gaulle thought every day of death and prepared to face it. He was convinced that an adversary of such stature would give prior warning of arrival. But instead it crept up behind him and he fell without a word onto the carpet, leaving his successor Pompidou unaware of the secret. De Gualle had also possessed the phial of the JL3 stolen on May 15, 1960, from Krushchev by Mr. Smith's men and retrieved by Colonel P. The four remaining chiefs of state did not know about this and so, after discussing the matter together, decided that since France was now unaware of the affair, it should be left in ignorance along with Germany.

Chapter 15

Jeanne finally fell asleep after her walk with Roland, the effects of the drug he had given her still not having worn off completely. But Roland couldn't sleep. Stretched out on his bed, his eyes closed, he recalled the Jeanne of old, a warm, ardent, childlike splendid Jeanne blooming like an August rose. When he had known that she was arriving, he had awaited her with an ever-increasing curiosity and tenderness. The same number of years had passed for both of them. He had forgotten that he hadn't changed. A man who looks at himself every morning while shaving and sees himself always the same, day after day for almost twenty years, couldn't possibly imagine the radical change that might occur in someone else over those years. He did imagine that age which should have marked him had probably made a few minor changes in her physique, that her face had probably acquired some vague wrinkles and signs of fatigue. But he had imagined all this in a sort of mist. He knew she would be surprised at first to find him unchanged, but he believed they would be happy and joyous at being together again and delight in telling each other everything that had happened during their separation.

And then the terrible thing had occurred: *he hadn't recognized her.*

He had remembered the August rose, but he found in front of him a different woman altogether, passionless and cold as a diamond hardened by fire. Where was the Jeanne of his memories? When she awakened in the morning, she would have recovered her capacity for suffering. He knew that he must not leave her alone for several days. But he also knew that by staying beside her, he was going to keep her pain alive. What could he do?

He got up. His thirty-two-year-year-old body behaved according to its usual habits and he telephoned Lony. She was alone, so he joined her. With her, he found again some of his animal insouciance, which was very pleasant. They made love, and she fell asleep. He looked at her as she lay on her side, revealing a lovely profile, young and beautiful, unblemished and graceful. He thought that what they had just done together—the agitation, the sighs, all that they had not wished with heart, soul and body as one but had desired by an instinct more powerful than that—was grotesque and humiliating. Was that the glory of creation, and they, this man and this woman, were they the kings of that creation, indulging in such gymnastics?

He tried to recall the rue de Vaugirard, the tenderness he had felt after he and Jeanne had made love, the calmness, his heart swollen with gentleness and gratitude, the perfumes of love, their sighs and whispers, their lovely sleep within a warm embrace.

But his memories vanished like mist, leaving him with a heartrending regret.

He too fell asleep. When he awoke in the morning, his qualms had disappeared. He and Lony made love once more, and while she was singing in the shower, he dressed and left. He didn't want to leave Jeanne all alone.

Chapter 16

In the month of June, 1972, the Duke of Windsor died and Mr. Kissinger flew to Peking. Jeanne awakened to her second morning on the Island completely panic-stricken.

President Pompidou was preparing for the Paris Summit meeting. His great problem was to strengthen Europe without relinquishing any of France's advantages, and not to let himself be "taken" by the United States without at least troubling the Americans. He knew nothing about the Island, nor did Prime Minister Heath, the German Chancellor Willy Brandt or any of the other nine delegates who were soon to meet in Paris. In England, Elizabeth II had refused the two small boxes that Samuel Frend had brought her. At that time, Frend knew nothing of real importance. He learned what the secret really was only when he arrived on the island. Then he understood the meaning of his mission.

Han and Annoa loved each other but didn't know how to say it since they had never been taught the words. He continued to tell her she was beautiful and she continued to laugh gaily. She was five months pregnant by now. Her concave little belly had become flat, then round like a soft, full cheek. There were now 1,467 inhabitants on the Island, of whom one-third were children from ten to eighteen years of age.

There was no social or political structure. Professor Hamblain's housekeeper earned the same salary as the professor—that is to say, nothing. She continued to do housework by habit and because she didn't know how to do anything else. She was happy to have stopped catching colds but didn't quite understand this tale about immortality and couldn't believe it was true. She said that one had to die one day or another. She missed her gossipy talks with the baker and the butcher and was slightly bored. She spent a great deal of time watching television.

No one governed, no one was in command. In each kind of work required, the most competent person was the one asked for help and ideas by the others. If a problem arose or an idea cropped up, someone spoke of it on the internal television circuit. Then others came to discuss it. Then the adults voted, adults being all those eighteen or over, since eighteen was the age when the person was "stabilized." The children were consulted and sometimes asked to vote if the decision concerned them. If the problem under examination demanded a program, a committe of volunteers was formed to take responsibility for it. When the program was terminated, the committee was dissolved.

On his arrival, Samuel Frend joined the Gilead Committee, charged with preparing the project of the same name. Project Gilead included two sections: the theoretical perfection of a long-distance rocket capable of carrying a great number of passengers and material; and the invention of a motor that would counterbalance gravity. Physicists who had come to the Island from the United States, China and France were working on this problem.

Alarming rumors were afloat regarding Mao's health and his political position. There was no denial by the Chinese, but it seemed that the rumors were no more well-founded than previous ones had been.

Chapter 17

Samuel Frend washed his face in cold water and dried his wet beard with a towel. Before leaving for the Island, not knowing who he might run across there from the old days, he had modified his physical appearance by shaving off the little hair he had left on his head and letting his mustache and beard grow. He was surprised to see that the beard was so white but noted that it did camouflage him perfectly.

The time he had spent perfecting his theoretical and practical knowledge now made it possible for him to have access to everything on the Island that would facilitate his mission.

He drank a cup of very hot coffee, and, dressed in a gray outfit that indicated his multiple talents, took the elevator to the exit room on the highest floor of the Citadel. Ever since a girl had once succeeded in taking a few steps outside without protection, the door guards had been doubled in number. Four volunteers were continually stationed next to each exit. Two were armed with machine guns. Two others were dressed in white dungarees resembling diving suits with similar protective helmets for wear on the exterior. Frend put on a white outfit and helmet. One of the guards locked it with a key and hung the key on the wall. No matter what happened, Frend would be unable to take off the helmet or the dungarees before his return into the Citadel. A bottle on his back furnished him with oxygen for breathing. If the people living on the Island had been permitted to breathe outside the Citadel, the virus would escape into the exterior atmosphere. The white diving outfit was not for their protection but to protect the outside world against them.

Frend took with him the satchel of tools he had prepared, hung it over his shoulder and entered his cylinderical chamber. When he closed the interior door, a shower sprayed him with a liquid containing a concentration of acid strong enough to destroy any microbes. He slid open the exterior door and went out into the middle of a thick gray fog that covered everything beyond his helmet. The platform he was standing on formed the bottom of a pit three meters in diameter cut into the rock. He walked with his hands outstretched before him and immediately found the first supporting beams for the antenna whose large iron arm rose above the Island. He climbed it and, as his head finally pierced through the fog's ceiling, he was blinded by the reflection of the sun. He had the impression that he was emerging from an immense cream puff.

The upkeep of the antenna was one of the responsi-

bilities he had taken over. This permitted him to graft
onto the pylon tower a tiny electronic device, a miniature of the same kind used in spaceships. This electronic
device served as a supplementary secret circuit which
added to the normal sending and receiving circuits of
the Island. It was cleverly disguised and seemed to be a
part of the antenna itself. He hadn't yet used it but
planned to do so within the next two hours. Then perhaps it would never have to be used again. He verified
that all the necessary connections were attached, and
then added the last missing piece, a platinum screw. Everything was ready and in order.

He threw back his head and looked through his helmet at the pale, cloudless sky. Then he looked at the pylon tower below, which pierced through the white cot-
tony fog. White and blue extended around him on all
sides. Frend was suspended between the two universes
and separated from both by the impassable shell of his
suit. He could smell neither the sea air nor the odor of
dust that is usual in heavy fogs, even those at sea. He
smelled the nylon, the oil of the respirator's valves and
his own sweat in spite of the lavender water he had
splashed on himself. He was attached to the universe of
the Island in his closed bubble by a tie stronger than any
steel cable, the JL3 that rendered him totally inter-
dependent with and committed to all the other inhabitants on the Island, sharing the same advantages and dis-
advantages. He knew that in the Citadel no one was
forced to do anything. That was true, except for the fact
that they didn't have the right to leave. The virus extended ad infinitum the time span of each life but reduced space to a hollow rock.

Suddenly, clinging to the green tower, lost in the im-
mensities of blue and white like an insect stuck to a leaf-
less stem rising out of a snowy desert, he was aware of
his solitude. He was no longer part of, would perhaps
never again be part of, that world stuffed with illusions

and hopes, peevish and miserable, that he pictured
dancing, fighting, laughing, weeping, dying and rotting
beyond the mist.

Far away to the southeast was the United States and
his family. By now, he probably had grandchildren. He
closed his eyes and held his breath for forty seconds
while he counted backward, exhaled, then began again.
This was a simple exercise that after years had become a
reflex he used to chase away the thought of his wife and
children. He knew nothing of what had happened to
them since his visit to the White House. Choosing to be
a man who had never had a family, he refused even to
accept news of them. He was now Samuel Bas, an
engineer without memories, who was responsible for a
secret mission handed to him by the four most powerful
heads of state in the world and who, in accomplishing
his mission, had been infected with immortality. Because
of what he had done and what he would have to do, he
could not call for his family. He had no past, he had
only a future that might turn out to be endless.

He descended and disappeared into the fog.

In his room, he closed the door and sat down before
a wall closet whose sliding door was open. He had made
a hidden niche in the back wall in which he had placed a
gray case. He took the case out of the recess and placed
it on his knees. A transmitting wire connected the case
to the lower part of the antenna that ran along the wall
inside the closet. Frend looked at his watch and saw it
was eleven-thirty. He had made a rendezvous for that
hour with Nixon, Brezhnev and Mao. The front of the case
facing him had six small bulbs, four white, one red and
one yellow. Three white bulbs lit up at half-second intervals. The red bulb lit up at the same time as the last
white one. The fourth white bulb did not light up. It was
the signal of Queen Elizabeth, who had declined the
rendezvous, and Frend had modified the case according-
ly.

Frend sighed and then pushed the yellow button, using the Morse code. The Morse code was one of the first things he had learned when he had become an agent. The word he sent for one minute was always the same —APPLE, APPLE, APPLE.

The antenna of the Island sent it, the satellite received it and amplified it. In the minute that followed, the listening post at the White House communciated the message to President Nixon. As soon as Nixon was informed, he telephoned the code word APPLE to Moscow and Peking. This was done to verify that Brezhnev and Mao had also received it. Everything was working as planned.

The listening posts of the heads of state received news of the Island at regular intervals. And even if these messages had been decoded by others, they would have meant nothing to someone not in on the secret. Sent out by radio from the Citadel, they were extremely brief and only gave general news. The foreign services that picked them up usually thought that the messages concerned atomic research being carried out on Islet 307.

Frend put the case back into the recess and connected it with a powerful compact transmitter already installed there. He verified everything once again, then closed up the recess and camouflaged it. He might never have to reopen it.

Mao had been up for a short time. At the end of a hard day, Brezhnev was going to bed. Nixon went to meet his wife for tea. Frend ate some lunch.

Chapter 18

The *Vendredi XIII* ("Friday the Thirteenth"), its three-pointed sails trained toward the stormy sky and flapping madly in the twisting wind, entered the surging seas of the Atlantic. The voice of the English announcer, his Oxford accent slightly broken by emotion, declared that this French boat could win the race of single-navigator ships from Plymouth, England, to Newport, America.

Han didn't know where either Plymouth or Newport were. He knew where the United States was but wasn't quite sure about England. The known geography of the world didn't interest him. When he leaned over the large and luminous globe of the world that turned slowly in the center of the screening room, it was the empty blue of the oceans that fascinated him. He placed his hand on their smooth surface, and his jaws tightened when he felt in his palm the warmth of the plastic.

When he ran his hand over Annoa's soft, round belly, he felt the same warmth and the same mystery. There, under his hand, was something other than what was obvious and visible—unknown life, unimaginable space, blood and infinite light.

The *Pen Duik Four* with its three shells came into view on the TV screen. Behind and in front of it was the ocean and then the horizon, stretching so far that its end could never be seen. But on the Island there was no horizon, except for that seen on the television screens.

Han rose, stretched his arms high and let out a cry like that of a deer ready to run through the forest in spring. Enormous earphones hid his ears so that he only heard his voice inside his head. His cry was mixed with the noise of the wind against the boat's sails on the other side of the earth.

There were fifty-two receiving sets in the room, gray or in color, placed everywhere so that it was possible to see only one or all at the same time. Earphones spread over the carpet like mushrooms lying on moss. Naked children, their ears covered by earphones, resting on the ground or sitting in armchairs, stools or on tree trunks, were crowded together before two groups of color TV sets. The sets were transmitting various programs, including a major automobile race, a motorcycle race across the Nevada desert and a police detective movie taking place in New York City. Cars, traffic jams, crowds, shootouts, clouds of dust and explosions were an unknown fabulous universe entering the eyes and ears of the children on the Island. There were those on the Island who declared from experience that such a universe really did exist outside the Island and that misery and death reigned there. But to the young children who didn't know what misery was and who only knew about death from images on the screens or fights between the animals in the gardens, it seemed a wonderful world full of mysterious delights. So they looked at the TV screens with fright and desire, relishing that universe of dream and nightmare. They had only to close their eyes to cease to believe in its existence.

Lying on the moss-colored carpet, Annoa listened but kept her eyes closed. She heard the wind and sea. They entered inside her and descended from her head into her belly, so that it became the sea and the sky. Han had entered there, and now the world was in her belly and growing.

Han lay down next to her. He put his arms around

her and clasped her gently against him. She smiled confidently and, rocking in his arms, fell calmly asleep to the sound of the sea.

Chapter 19

Jeanne took tranquilizers to protect herself against the pain of her disappointment. But she couldn't protect herself against her own indifference to everything surrounding her. Neither the inhabitants nor the experiments and experiences of the Island interested her.

Loving Roland, she had discovered an extraordinary joy whose existence she hadn't even suspected before, the joy of seeing, hearing, savoring everything together. Because they looked as one at the apparent banalities of the world, doors opened before them to reveal hidden splendors.

Those doors had closed in Jeanne's face the night of the fire at Villejuif. For seventeen years she had traveled over the world without really seeing it, living only in the hope that she was finally going to find Roland and that everything would be as before.

But in the second she had found him, that hope died. Roland had become living proof of the presence of the impossible.

She would have preferred not to see him anymore, but it was he who came to her with an air of assurance and at the same time with anxiety and unease in his eyes. And when he didn't come to her, she couldn't stop herself from going to him, staring at the image of his intact youth, suffering like a mother who looks constantly at the photograph of her dead son thinking that if he were alive, how he would have changed.

Each day, the moment she saw him again was as agonizing as the first time. He was so much the same as when she had loved him, as she had guarded his image in her memory, her heart, her mind and her very flesh, that she felt a fantastic desire to throw herself in his arms, to cry and laugh, to embrace and kiss, to forget what she had become while he remained unchanged, to believe the unbelievable, to dream.

But she was a woman with a clear, lucid mind. She always looked carefully at herself in the mirror before leaving her room. And when she was with Roland, she saw superimposed on him her own image framed by the rectangular sides of the mirror, the pane of glass that was incapable of reflecting other than the glaring truth.

To give herself courage, she murmured to herself the words he had once said, idiotic and marvelous words of love that terrified her when applied to her now, such as "my rose, my flower, my garden, the most beautiful." This made her laugh, and everything seemed somehow better.

Day after day, week after week, with the help of pills, she became inured to spending hours in his company, leaving him and then meeting him again, like a brother, a friend, a dream lover, an old comrade with whom one has crossed the desert and the gardens of Babylon. They understood each other perfectly, they still had the same tastes and judgments, but there was no longer the least intimacy between them, because intimacy is finally sensual.

Jeanne had tried to keep busy, to integrate herself into one of the groups that was carrying out new kinds of scientific research. But nothing interested her. This world, whose first preoccupation, originality and function was to live eternally, was foreign to her. Life for her was no longer of any importance. On the contrary, what did bring her a kind of tranquillity was the fact that she seemed to be immune to the JL3 virus. The first few nights she had waited in vain for symptoms of contamination, for the flaming red signs in the night. But nothing happened and she began to hope that nothing would happen and that she would continue to grow older. Time would finally put out the flames of regret and pain that still remained. While Roland stayed young, she would continue to slowly age and thus move away from him imperceptibly like a ship that at last glance disappears peacefully over the horizon. But she knew it was possible that the virus would invade her system at any moment and keep her "stabilized."

Naturally, the biologists and the doctors on the Island had tried, under the direction of Bahanba, to find an antidote to the JL3. If such an antidote could be found, humanity might perhaps make use of immortality rather than simply suffer its consequences. But the work of Hamblain, Galdos, Ramsay, Roland and their Russian and Chinese colleagues had yielded no results as yet. The JL3 which had vanquished cancer, previously an incurable disease, and had made death retreat, in turn showed itself to be resistant to any attempt to control it. Galdos had discovered a vaccine he called C41 that had raised hopes because it kept rats from catching the virus for six months. But it had no effect on monkeys. Ears of corn began to sprout, but the grains remained as small as peppercorns and didn't ripen. Rice and wheat remained totally untouched by the treatment and continued to produce only flowers. A tomato plant had produced fruit for two years and then, when sprayed with the JL3, began to flower again. Three aged dogs and cats had been imported from Europe and treated with the C41 vaccine on their arrival. In spite of the vaccine, the cats had become contaminated with the JL3 virus within the usual time limit. But the dogs, on the other hand, had reacted well to it, continuing to age like any dog in the world. Even direct injections of the JL3 had not stopped the process. The female died of a breast tumor after months of illness, the male cocker spaniel died of a heart attack and the poodle of pneumonia.

The question now was, What would be the effect of the C41 on man? Experiments on animals and plants did not provide solid scientific proof. But it was difficult to propose such an experiment to a newcomer not yet infected with the JL3 virus, because in agreeing to be a guinea pig, he might lose his chance for immortality.

When Jeanne learned from Roland about the existence of the C41 and its effect on the dogs, she asked to be vaccinated.

Chapter 20

Jeanne went with Han and Annoa to the stable to view the newest curiosity on the Island, a white buffalo. Frend, who happened to be there at the time, was caught by surprise as they entered and took care to keep his back to Jeanne as he hurriedly left. In any case, Jeanne paid no special attention to him.

The animal's odor, mixed with the fake country smells, and the chimes of a village bell gave the illusion of a pasture on a spring afternoon. Jeanne was taken aback by the color of the gigantic buffalo's fur. It had become white, the animal as gentle as a lamb, probably due either to the massive doses of female hormones given it daily to suppress its sexual impulses or to one of the anti-JL3 vaccines injected into it for experimental purposes. Since there was no hay available on the Is-

land, it ate with apparent enjoyment the daisies, butter-
cups, orchids and rose petals that had become its daily
fare. Dr. Galdos was anxious to learn why the buffalo's
fur had lost is pigmentation. One day its eyes had begun
to turn blue and its fur white, and within six months it
resembled an overgrown, humpbacked, uncurled lamb
with forget-me-not eyes.

When Jeanne entered with Han and Annoa, the beast
was lying down in the middle of the large round stable
looking like a Mayan pyramid, with small children
climbing playfully up its flanks. In the buffalo's eyes
was a dreamy look of nostaliga for the days when it had
galloped on the unbounded plains with its brothers. It
rose gently and shook itself like a wet dog, making the
children tumble to the ground with cries of pleasure. It
turned to stare at Jeanne with a melancholy air. She
couldn't believe it possible. But what did the words
"possible" and "impossible" mean in a place like this?

Jeanne had found some interest in life by taking Annoa under her wing. Han and Annoa, so innocent and
pure, so adoring and passionate, reminded her of the
joyful moments in the past when she and Roland had
forgotten family, work and duties to meet and make
love together as though the world were just beginning.

She recalled how she had suffered in giving birth to
her son and was determined that such pain should be
spared the golden girl who carried her little belly thrust
out before her with pride and amusement, never imagin-
ing what was in store. Jeanne had assisted at natural
childbirth deliveries and had found the experience exhil-
arating. How could women have been left to such fear
and suffering over the centuries when giving birth could
be such a profound joy for the mother?

Gynecology wasn't her specialty, so she asked Roland
to send to France for books on the subject. A week later, one arrived by way of the Island's teletype, which re-

ceived and immediately transcribed the text and illustrations.

Han had climbed on the back of the buffalo, while a group of boys and girls raced after the animal, hanging onto its tail as it trotted around the circular wall bellowing happily. Suddenly, the buffalo let itself fall down in the center of the stable and lay on its stomach. The ground trembled, and the naked children, exhausted with joy, fell to the ground also. There was a moment of silence during which Jeanne heard a strange drone she had noticed several times before when the noise on the Island had occasionally stopped.

"What's that humming sound?" Jeanne asked Annoa.

"That's the lung!" answered Annoa, surprised at Jeanne's ignorance.

Chapter 21

On November 8, 1960, John Fitzgerald Kennedy was elected President of the United States. On January 20, 1961, when he actually entered office, and after all the official ceremonies were ended, former President Eisenhower told his successor about the existence of the JL3 virus and the community living on Islet 307. Kennedy was both amazed and delighted despite the mortal danger it contained. Having experienced so much pain himself, he understood what a marvelous promise of hope the virus held out to humanity. He had been severely wounded in World War II, when his spine had been almost cut in two. The surgeons had performed a lumbar disk operation and in 1954 he had undergone another operation, this one for the insertion of a steel plate, that he had barely survived. Since then, he had lived strapped tightly into an iron corset. It was this corset that obliged the killers to aim at his head when they assassinated him in Dallas.

But on the evening of January 20, 1961, Kennedy had no suspicion of the tragic end awaiting him in Dallas. And in addition to the enormous task of leading the most powerful nation in the world, he learned of the important part he was to play as one of those responsible for saving humanity from deadly peril. Eisenhower told him about Khrushchev's fears concerning a possible leak of the JL3 virus outside the Island and of his project to send man into outer space.

Kennedy was extremely enthusiastic about the project. It fitted beautifully into his slogan, "The New Frontier." He decided to meet with Khrushchev as soon as possible to coordinate their efforts and avoid losing time and money.

From the fifth to the eighth of April, he received Prime Minister Macmillan of England, and the next week he saw German Chancellor Adenauer. Kennedy asked both of them if Europe would take part in the space program. Macmillan did not suspect the gravity of the problem as Adenauer did, but both responses were negative.

De Gaulle had not been able to come to Washington because of the Algerian crisis, so Kennedy met with him in Europe on May 31. De Gaulle had seen Adenauer in Bonn ten days earlier. He confirmed what Adenauer and Macmillan had said—that the expenses demanded by the space program were too high for European budgets, even if they were united. De Gaulle profoundly regretted the absence of Europe and above all of France in this venture, but he had to bow before the enormous weight of the costs entailed.

When Kennedy found himself facing Khrushchev in

Vienna on June 3, the situation was clear. The two great nations were to go it alone in their pioneer work in the development of future space programs. At Vienna on June 3 and 4, 1961, the most fantastic secret agreement in human history was made, dividing the solar system into two zones of influence. Vienna became the Yalta of space.

But Kennedy and Khrushchev were not Roosevelt and Stalin. At the beginning of a more peaceful era than that of their predecessors, and fearful of the consequences of the JL3 virus, they had both decided not to project political differences outside the orbit of Earth. They had setteld on a division of responsibilities rather than imperialism. The decision was made that the moon would first be explored by both the Soviet Union and the United States, such explorations serving moreover as testings of men and materials with a view to voyages further on into outer space.

The immediacy of the JL3 peril demanded that those planets capable of sustaining human life be surveyed rapidly. The U.S. took responsibility for the exploration of Mars and the U.S.S.R. of Venus. It was obvious to the world that the space programs of Russia and America were not competitive but complementary. And the agreement survived the two leaders even when, after their deaths, the United States began exploring Mars and the Soviet Union explored Venus. Eleven years later, the results were as follows:

The leading scientists of the world, including those on the Island, analyzed the rock samples and dust brought back from the Moon by American astronauts and Soviet robots.

It was discovered that the moon has no air, water or any kind of animal or vegetable alimentation. Nothing, only rocks. Could men eventually eat, drink and breathe by means of those rocks?

The answer was yes. The lunar boulders contain all the material necessary for the fabrication of air, water and synthetic nourishment.

A plan provided for "sowing" the moon. Drilling and converting machines in attendant parts would be placed on the moon by pilotless rockets, making use of Russian techniques, and would then be followed by men, making use of American techniques, who would assemble the machines and start them working. They would dig themselves in under the lunar soil and create an insulated oxygenated interior in which machines could function and men lie, taking their subsistence from the rock in which they would be enclosed. Other similar stations would be created in the area. then joined and enlarged and made into a single station. The process would be repeated at multiple points until enough gravity had been manufactured on the surface of the satellite to secure an exterior atmosphere, water and eventually life.

This program would require a great deal of time, perhaps centuries, a major part of world budgets and untapped sources of energy.

The amount of money needed would impose sacrifices on man that only the threat of a known peril could justify. The threat of the JL3 virus was such a peril. The chiefs of the states engaged in the space program felt certain that a world educated to the potentially terrible effects of the virus would eagerly accept the sacrifices necessary for the space program.

But a serious problem remained—no machine could function on the moon or elsewhere without energy. During fourteen days out of twenty-eight, the moon receives an incalculable and inexhusitible quantity of solar energy. Therefore, it was urgently necessary to learn how to make use of solar energy. The British, French, German, American, Russian and Chinese governments gave instructions to their research scientists with this goal in mind. But in almost all these nations, the great oil companies used their power, secretly or openly, to oppose this work either by legal or illegal means. Researchers everywhere came up against diverse materials, financial, administrative or "accidental" obstacles.

By the end of 1970, an English physicist and a French electronics expert who were working together on this problem were just about ready to perfect a technique for transforming solar rays into electric current. The physicist came to Paris to join his French colleague. They left on December 29 in the latter's car for a country house he had inherited near Cassis in the south of France, believing that the winter sun of Provence would be most useful for the last stage of their work.

The Frenchman's car, a cream-colored Citroen D.S., was blocked for six hours one night near Avignon by a snowstorm that immobilized thousands of automobiles on the superhighway going through the Rhone Valley.

The two men remained in their car, not daring to leave their records and material. The cold and snow continued for hours, and in the middle of the night, the Frenchman decided to go and look for food, hot coffee and blankets in the nearest village.

He was found the next day in a ditch with a broken leg, frozen to death. The English physicist, half-frozen and unconscious, was taken from the car to the hospital. When he recovered and learned of his colleague's death, he tried to retrieve the records and other material that had been left in the trunk of the car, but he couldn't locate the cream-colored Citroen anywhere. He returned to London, traumatized by his experience, entered a hospital for psychiatric treatment and died there eleven days later, seemingly from an overdose of drugs.

In the Russian Ilyushin that crashed near Moscow in July, 1972, one of the passengers was the physicist Blagomirov, on his way from the Crimea with his records, instruments and samples of combinations of alloys, which, arranged in a certain order, produced electric current when exposed to the sun. Everything burned and melted in the plane's flames.

On January 16, 1971, sixteen oil companies formed a cartel to oppose the demands of the Arab countries producing the "black gold." Such a front had always existed in secret everywhere in the world against anything that might threaten the oil interests, the difference now being that they had come out in the open. Oil has its ministers in all governments, and most of the secret services unknowingly work for it. Oil is a power in itself. reigning over all economies, including those of the socialist countries. It provokes wars from Biafra to Sinai, it kills, imprisons, corrupts. Siva's blood is oil, Bahanba declared. A Christian would have called it the devil's blood.

Because of lack of money and energy, the lunar project remained in its preliminary stages. The United States suspended its Apollo program, and the Soviet Union slowed down its lunar experiments.

The U.S.S.R. succeeded in piercing the thick blanket of clouds that had prevented any observation of the planet Venus. The sounding line sent some brief information by radio before being mysteriously destroyed. This information indicated that Venus's atmosphere is composed of poisonous gasses and that its temperature reaches 600 degrees. Soviet exploration of Venus will continue until there is a certainty that that planet is unfit for human life.

The United States placed several observer satellites around the planet Mars. In November, 1972, some conclusions drawn from data recorded by the instruments were made public: life could have existed once and might still exist on Mars, doubtless in forms that are different and more primitive than those on earth. The secret conclusion has been that it would be as difficult for man to settle on Mars as on the moon.

For the first time in the history of known astronomical observations and perhaps for the first time in the history of humanity, near the end of the 1980s almost all the planets will be in conjunction with each other, that is to say, they will be aligned one after the other on the same side of the sun. The slow, heavy planets at the extreme end of the solar system are already on their way toward this extraordinary rendezvous. At the moment when they will be closest to each other, their influences will be superimposed one on the other, and the earth will be torn between their consequent increased attraction and that of the sun. It is quite possible that unusual climatic changes will occur and that the earth's orbit will be affected.

Astrologists have pointed out that only the planet Jupiter will be located on the other side of the earth. Jupiter represents established order, things as they are. Order and stability will thus be in opposition to all influences. The greatest astrologists in the world foresee considerable changes for mankind during this period. Elizabeth II's private astrologist told her about such fears for the future. The Queen asked many questions, trying to learn if the changes to occur would possibly result from the JL3 virus. But it was impossible to find that out without asking revealing questions, so she received no satisfactory answer.

The United States has sent a rocket into space that will profit from the alignment of the exterior planets and pass near all of them. It will send back information for twenty years. Then, having passed Pluto, it will move off into the galactic void before returning centuries later as an obscure comet, its message no longer of any value.

In spite of all the scientific knowledge employed and money spent, the space program is still only a pioneer effort. The Big Four involved with the secret of Islet 307 were certain of only one thing—much time will be needed before man can leave his cradle for the hostile environment of space. It was therefore important to ensure that there would be no way the least trace of the virus could escape from the Island.

Chapter 22

Jeanne had started by giving lessons in natural childbirth to Annoa in the girl's room. Han attended them too. After several sessions, a number of children came in to watch what was going on. There were finally so many children clustered about the room that it became impossible to do the exercises. There was no question of closing the door or otherwise keeping the children out. They went where they wished, were their own masters. The adults gave them advice and taught them, but did not give orders.

To simplify things, Jeanne decided to hold the sessions in the round garden. By the tenth session, all the children on the Island were there, lying on the grass or sitting in the trees, listening and trying to imitate the movements and exercises she was teaching Annoa. The naked children were extremely beautiful, but they formed so thick and dense a crowd that Jeanne began to suffer from claustrophobia. She cut short the lesson and returned to her own room.

There were too many adults and youngsters on the Island for the volume of space they occupied. Except when she visited the lower levels of the Island, which were occupied by the machines, Jeanne couldn't take a step anywhere without being surrounded by walls of people that opened and closed around her.

The Island's crowded streets resembled the Paris subway at the end of a working day. Happily, the people here didn't run, shove or have the haggard look on their faces worn by the workers of the outside world as they hurried between their work and their home, forever racing toward the end of their life. The Islanders were not indifferent but rather relaxed, delivered from cares and tribulations. Their attitude was neither aggressive nor indifferent, and one always met another with a smile or an intimate look. But it was still a crowd. Sometimes Jeanne felt a crazy desire to shove everyone aside and run alone. But that was impossible since the Citadel was like a full bottle. And the crowd in the streets was only a part of the whole. There were always people indoors, busy with tasks of one sort or another.

What kept Jeanne from suffocating was the ever-present breeze and the lovely sound of the bells. The breeze and the bells made the ceiling and walls seem to disappear, as though at the next turning one would find a familiar open landscape.

"There are too many of you," she said to Roland. "You shouldn't have had so many children. When they double in size and volume, you are going to burst."

Roland had come to give her another dose of the C41. She drank it in a glass of water mixed with honey.

Roland smiled and replied, *We're* going to burst. You said 'you,' but now you are a part of us."

She shook her head and answered quietly, "No."

No, she was not a part of them. For that to happen, it would be necessary for the chasm between her and Roland to close. And at each step Roland made toward her, she drew back. She lived on the Island, she knew she couldn't leave it, but she had been catapulted into it like a projectile, and she remained there like a foreign body. The solution lay perhaps in these drops of culture medium that would permit her to slowly escape from the torture of her memories, to move step by step away from the temptation of the impossible and to leave the Island by the only door permitted—if it would only rest ajar, at least for her—the aging process and, finally, death.

"I've been here for three months and six days and I still haven't seen the color red at night."

"Are you pleased about that?"

"Yes."

Roland rose from the armchair and began to pace up and down the room.

"You'd be happy to grow old and die?"

"I have grown old. And I'm not happy. That's all."

"But I too . . ."

He fell silent. Obviously it was not true. He had grown older in years, but he had not aged.

"However, it seems to me that *you* are the younger of the two of us, Jeanne. I know that perhaps one day I'll be a thousand years old, and I feel as though I have reached that age already. While you, you're still fragile as a little girl who catches colds and the flu in the world outside. Jeanne!"

He held out his hands and bent over her. She didn't move but looked at him from head to foot, her heart ice-cold so that she could stifle the flame of hope lighted from time to time by a word or gesture from Roland.

"Don't be an idiot," she said.

"It's you who are the idiot," Roland replied.

He sat down next to her on the bed and tenderly put his arm around her. She felt her heart leap, tried to disengage herself, lost courage, closed her eyes and leaned her head against his shoulder.

"Roland, Roland, please. It's not possible. You know that. You'll always remember me as I was then."

He tried to answer, but there was nothing left to say. But he couldn't forget precisely what he was trying to

recapture by holding her in his arms. She, Jeanne, was
there, but where was the Jeanne he remembered? In order to love Jeanne, he had first to forget her.

He stopped trying to convince himself and her. He
leaned on her and she on him, each with their own separate hurt and with their common pain. They were quiet,
almost content. Some part of their old intimacy had
been reborn from the consolation of being together, the
warmth of their bodies mingling and their wordless understanding of each other. Jeanne opened her eyes and
looked at the blank wall on which each occupant could
paint what he wished. Jeanne had painted nothing. The
wall was white, as though waiting. Through the door
that she had purposely left open, two lovely butterflies
were wafted into the room by the breeze. They danced
and quivered in the air, tossed slowly about like flowers,
a blue flame and a brown, lovingly entwined as the light
breeze carried them away again.

Chapter 23

When he went to work in the radio room, Den
wore the first pair of overalls that he could find on the
shelf. Today he put on an orange pair, slightly too big
and too long for him.

The radio room was large and rectangular, the back
wall entirely covered by radio transmitters for communicating with the outside world, teletype machines and television sets open to all channels. Perpendicular to the
two high walls, workbenches were set up for studying,

repairs, research. Aided by two girls and a boy, all younger than himself, Den was putting together a radio transmitter of his own invention. It would send messages anywhere in the world, no matter how far away. It would weigh practically nothing, and would transmit on a hundred wavelengths at once. Den had solved innumerable techincal problems that he didn't even know were problems any more than he realized that he was a genius.

"When we leave with Project Gilead, this will be our radio equipment. Not exactly the same one, though. I'm going to make another smaller set," Den explained.

"You'll go in Gilead?" asked the small boy.

"Of course."

"Where will you go?"

"I don't know. Far away."

"To the moon?"

"Oh, farther than that, I hope."

"To the sun?"

"That's not possible, because it would burn us up."

"To Zimponpon?"

"What's Zimponpon?"

"It's a star I invented that's farther away than anything else in the universe," replied the small boy.

"Yes, then perhaps I'll go to Zimponpon."

"Will you take me along?"

"Of course."

"And will I be grown up when I get back?"

"Once we reach Zimponpon, we won't ever return."

"Why?"

"We won't want to, because it will be so beautiful."

The flat screen of the interior television service lit up on the ceiling, and Bahanba's face appeared. Throughout the Island, the entire population, silent and immobile, listened intently as Bahanba announced that he was going to die.

Chapter 24

Jeanne and Roland strolled through the Island. "The wind carries them away, but where to?" Jeanne asked.

"Come and see."

They continued to cross the Island and, as they advanced, saw an increasing number of butterflies as well as bees and other colorful insects being carried away like snowflakes by the light breeze. When tired, the insects sometimes settled on human beings or clung to the walls and ceiling. As soon as they began to fly again, the obstinate breeze took them up gently and carried them away once more. Roland explained the reason for this.

"The Island can't run the risk of the JL3 germs being blown outside by a draft of wind, through an open door or even a crack. The first inhabitants of the Island immediately installed a large ventilator, and others were added later. They operate day and night, creating a constant air flow inside the Island. Air from outside enters by way of the tiniest apertures, or by wide-open doors when we open them to let the barges enter, but the air from inside cannot get out. We're nearing the ventilators. Can you hear them?"

They stopped. In spite of the familiar noise of the crowd, Jeanne heard the purring sound that had sometimes surprised her when the Island was otherwise silent.

"It's the Island's lung," Ronald explained.

"But a lung inhales and exhales. The air that's breathed in must be breathed out."

166

"You'll see what happens."

They went on to where the street changed and became a narrow corridor, with the ceiling becoming progressively lower. The light breeze turned into a strong wind. The insects spattered against the walls like pieces of hail, and the wind carried away what was left of their bodies. Vertical bars closed the end of the corridor at the spot where it opened obliquely into a much larger corridor. Through the bars, Jeanne saw other similar openings in the opposite wall. A multicolored snowstorm of insects flew forth from all the openings. The insects were picked up by a draft of turbulent air and thrown horizontally into a whirlwind that was turning faster and faster. They disappeared at a terminal point that Jeanne was unable to see. The roar of the ventilators was now very near, and the wind sounded as though it were being inhaled and exhaled through the throat of a giant. Jeanne became short of breath, as though her lungs were being pulled out along with the butterflies and other insects into an increasingly powerful vortex.

"They are being blown into the fire," Roland shouted. "Come!"

He snatched her away from the bars and they left the area, bent over against the wind, which quickly subsided and finally turned into a light, caressing breeze that ruffled their hair.

Roland continued:

"The ventilators breathe in all the air from the entire Island and in the process gather up any insects along the way. Then the air is discharged outside the Island after passing through the fire inside a range of pipes twenty meters long, where the temperature reaches over a thousand degrees. No microbe, no germ of any kind can withstand it. In a thousandth of a second, the butterflies become sparks and ashes, then nothing.

"The adult females lay eggs constantly, so each day

several hundreds of millions of insects fly through the Island. We've imported all sorts of insect-eating birds, but they aren't enough. The wind takes care of the rest. As to crawling insects, those in the ground and walls, we've saturated everything on the Island with DDT, HCH and five or six similar poisons. Also, we had to inundate with acid and dry with blowpipes the entire underpinnings of the Island where ants had appeared from God knows where.

"Despite all the cleaning and washing given him, the buffalo brought fleas when he arrived. Not many, just about a dozen. But three weeks later, the Island was black with them. They climbed up around our ankles and all the furry animals scratched themselves unmercifully. We put a new insecticide, TCD, into the drinking water. Everyone drank it, including the animals, so that it entered the bloodstream. All the fleas that stung and drank blood died, and those that didn't sting ate dust and leavings filled with DDT and HCH. We finally succeeded in exterminating them.

"But the battle against the insects remains a permanent and frightening problem. Everything we eat, drink, breathe and touch on the Island is soaked in insecticide. Without it, we would have been overcome and destroyed. Of course, insecticides are also poisonous for man. But until now, neither we nor the animals have felt any ill effects from them. This might be due to the virus. I don't know. At any rate, the white pills you take each day counteract them.

"The other animals multiply to such a degree that we can't accommodate all of them on the Island either. We've tried to create a natural equilibrium, with each species of animal eating another species, but there are usually too many that survive. The greatest destroyer, the only reliable one for maintaining a proper equilibrium in nature, is death from old age or an epidemic. But here such things do not exist, so we have to intervene. Look!"

Roland showed Jeanne a closed grille with rails passing underneath it.

"Each night we send surplus animals to the fire via those rails. Usually we choose only young animals and birds' eggs. But from time to time, we have to sacrifice full-grown animals in order to keep the species in balance. They pass first into a room where they breath in gas that puts them quietly and painlessly to sleep. Then they are carried off to the flames. After that, nothing remains of them.

"Everything that leaves the Island must pass through the fire. Used water, drainage, waste and refuse, all wood, plastic, steel objects that have become useless, even barges, crates and wrappings, pass through temperatures that reach from one to three thousand degrees before they blow away as gas and steam into the fog or fall liquefied into the ocean.

"All that is done to keep one single bacillus, even a millionth of a millimeter, from escaping into the outside world."

Chapter 25

Roland and Jeanne had just reached a tree-lined square with three fountains when Bahanba's image appeared on the mural television screens.

"I want you all to listen to me carefully, above all the children. I am going to die."

Roland stopped and squeezed Jeanne's arm tightly. The other adults stopped also and fell silent. They looked at Bahanba's face, intent on catching each syllable he pronounced. They couldn't understand what he meant. On the Island, the sentence they had just heard made no sense. The weight of those words, which had oppressed men for an eternity, had fallen from their shoulders on arriving here. And yet the very man who had delivered them from that horror was taking it back on his shoulders again.

The children resumed their play because those words had never had any meaning for them. But Bahanba addressed them again insistently.

"Listen to me, my children."

They stopped then, and the birds sat still on the trees and around the fountains as though they understood. Someone pressed on a stone in a wall, and the waters in the fountains stopped running. The only sound was the distant murmur of the Island's lung. Bahanba smiled gently and with a slight weariness.

"I have gone beyond the length of life allotted to a man who has fought and suffered in the world outside ours. Today I think that, like those men, I have earned the right to leave. The virus that I imprudently discovered, although perhaps it was Vishnu the Preserver who so wished it, makes it impossible for me to die naturally. And I don't have the right to end my life with arms or to poison this body that has been loaned to me by the gods. But I can stop it by ceasing to feed the mysterious motors that make it move, repair itself and continue to function. This evening I am going to begin to fast once again, and I shall continue to do so until my body frees my spirit. I want you to become used to the idea that I am leaving, so that at the moment when my death occurs, you will not be demoralized or unhappy.

"I am no longer going to eat but will continue to drink water to wash me clean of impurities and keep my body going until my flesh has wasted away. I think this will probably take several weeks, perhaps two months or even longer. I hope to be conscious until the end. I ask you, the adults, not to profit from the weakness that will surely overtake me by giving me forced feedings, but instead to respect my wishes and not intervene. I ask you, the children, to come and see me.

"In a moment, when I finish speaking to you, I will bathe, then stretch out on my bed and will no longer move. Do not come today, but starting tomorrow, visit me in small groups. Speak to me softly. I may or may not answer, but I shall be with you. And you will see a peaceful death come to me. It is best that you know how life ends in that world that is no longer yours. You know only the fierce face of death, the animals devoured, accidents, war, murders that you have seen on the TV screens. But there is also a natural death that some believe to be an end, but that for me means a new beginning. Death can be very gentle for those who know how to accept it without fear as an inevitable consequence of life. I hope that mine will be like that. I ask that when I am dead, my body be given to the fire and that you rejoice on that day because I will be happy.

"My children, you must love, you must love everything."

Bahanba's voice stopped, and the TV screens all over the Island died out.

Chapter 26

The children again fasted along with Bahanba. They made a great effort to fast longer this time, and the eldest kept to it for three days. They weren't sad because they didn't understand what death meant—that is to say, the sudden definitive absence of someone. It was impossible for them to imagine that Grand-Ba was really going to disappear and that they would miss him. On the Island, everyone was always there. The adults remained the same day after day without any sign of physical or mental weakening, of a descent toward the end of life. Death only existed for them on the television screens, and they assumed that when the film was over, the people came to life again. If Grand-Ba had decided to die, it was because he was the most intelligent of them all and knew how to do what the others didn't dare to try. And then he had told them that he would be happy, so the children were gay. In the evening, they sang, danced and played in the gardens.

As soon as they heard that the children were going to fast, the adults warned them about making love during the period when they abstained from food. Late on the first day, Dr. Fuller, an American surgeon, appeared on the interior channel of the TV screens and explained to the children that a woman in the habit of taking birth-control medication, as they all did on the Island when eating their meals, would become extremely fertile if she stopped for a single day. He told the girls that if they didn't want what happened to Annoa to happen to them, they should stay away from the boys or else eat their meals.

This was unfortunate advice to give to the girls. They found what had happened to Annoa absolutely marvelous. Many who had not fasted the first day began to do so the following day, and they all made love with the boys continually.

On the second night, Han was lying down in the grass of the round garden next to Annoa. He placed his ear against Annoa's round belly, then leaped up and shouted, "I can hear it! I can hear it!"

As the children began to cluster around them, he once again placed his ear against Annoa's belly, murmuring "I can hear it" over and over again. Then he moved away to let the other children, one after another kneel and listen. And they heard inside Annoa the faint rapid beating of a heart that wasn't hers. Awestruck, they kept repeating: "It has a heart. It has a heart!"

Chapter 27

On August 1, 1963, President Kennedy held a press conference during which he discussed Berlin, whose security he wished guaranteed by Moscow; France, to which he refused to reveal atomic secrets if it did not return to active participation in NATO; South Africa, to which the United States would no longer furnish arms because of its racial policies; and the signing in the near future of a treaty concerning limitations on nuclear tests; and other less important matters.

As usual, the journalists asked him a great number of

questions. He answered rapidly, with no hesitation and coming directly to the point, a pleasant smile on his face. Actually, he was suffering badly from back pains. Each movement of the torso was torture for him. But he had already shown on other occasions his faculty for withstanding terrible pain.

Kennedy used both hands to get up from his armchair, always showing the cameras the image of an optimistic young President, yesterday's victor who must be tomorrow's as well. The Presidential elections were being held in a little over a year, and in several months he planned to begin his campaign for reelection.

He left the White House press room for his private apartments, where his doctors were waiting. They showed him the X-rays: the steel disk inserted into his spinal column had caused an inflammation of the two vertebra against which it lay. This inflammation was not only painful, but it might turn into an infection. The President must remember that he was overworked, and if he continued at the present pace, something very serious might happen to him.

The doctors prescribed antibiotics against infection, a painkiller and an immediate and prolonged rest. They knew he probably wouldn't listen to them and warned him that, if he didn't, the pain and the illness would finally condemn him to a longer, more permanent rest.

Two weeks later, new X-rays showed that the inflammation had completely disappeared. The doctors found him in almost perfect condition. He was no longer suffering at all and spoke of taking off his iron corset. His doctors dissuaded him, while congratulating him on the extraordinary vitality that had helped him to overcome his illness with the help, of course, of the treatment they had prescribed. They recommended, however, that he not overwork and that he rest as much as possible. He laughed and promised to do so.

When Samuel Frend, who knew more about it, arrived on the Island and eventually discovered its secret, he evolved a theory that answered many questions left in the dark during his Dallas inquiry. It was only a hypothesis, and it was fantastic. In order to confirm it, he had to obtain from Dr. Galdos certain information that, as it turned out, Galdos never really gave him. Frend, as a good agent, arranged to meet Galdos and become friendly with him. One evening, seated on the edge of the beach on the heights of the Citadel, Galdos seemed very relaxed and open, talking with some melancholy and nostalgia of his university, his students and his work before coming to the Island. Frend told him that he knew Harvard well, which made Galdos even more expansive, and Frend finally dared ask. "Did you receive the JL3 directly from Bahanba?"

"Yes, I was the one who identified and photographed it first, with a new electronic microscope. I almost missed seeing it, since I never expected such a tiny virus."

"I wonder if there isn't some JL3 lying around somewhere in the world outside. Did you really destroy all of it at Harvard?"

Galdos's face closed up completely.

"Of course, what a foolish question!"

"Yes, I know, but if I had been you, I think I would have given the President a phial. After all, it's hard to know what might happen. Imagine if Mao had it, or the Russians? What year did you leave the United States? Who was President then?"

"Eisenhower. I would have been crazy to do that," replied Galdos, who rose and left.

Frend attached as much importance to the way his questions were answered as he did to the answers themselves. Galdos's tone made him doubt he had been told the truth.

Frend knew what errors could be committed in the name of scientific passion or patriotism, and even more so by the two combined. He was convinced that the scientists to whom Bahanba had originally revealed the properties of the JL3 had hurried to their laboratories to verify the extraordinary declarations they had just heard. Before they had left for Islet 307, some of them, thinking of the future of science and their country, might have entrusted one precious and dangerous sample to the only other person who was in on the secret, the head of their country.

If Galdos, before embarking with his collaborators on the plane that was to "mysteriously" disappear in transit, had given a phial of the JL3 virus to Eisenhower, then many things could be explained.

Chapter 28

Immediately after the inauguration on January 20, 1961, Eisenhower not only revealed the secret of the JL3 to Kennedy but also gave him the phial that Dr. Galdos had presented to him in 1955. Kennedy put it away in a secret coffer in the White House and forgot about it.

After two years of handling innumerable crises and the exhaustion resulting from them, his back pains had become intolerable. The pain-killers offered him only short periods of respite. He remembered that his doctors had given him the choice between immediate rest and the threat of disaster. He took a double dose of his pain-killer and sat down to think over the situation. He couldn't take a rest. He also couldn't abide the idea of becoming helplessly crippled and being forced to give up his office at a time when the new national, world and even planetary policy he had initiated was in full momentum. A solution had to be found. He studied the record Eisenhower had given him as well as the reports arriving daily from Islet 307. He knew that part of the overall effect of the JL3 was to increase the natural defenses of an organism. He also knew the biologists on the Island were working ceaselessly to find an antidote for the virus. Perhaps they would discover a vaccine within months, weeks, even days.

In 1963, the American and Russian lunar programs were still far from reaching their objective. Both countries had allocated extremely large budgets to this research. Khrushchev and Kennedy were well aware that the moon was not the Ukraine or California and that farms could not be established there within any foreseeable future. But they did ask themselves if perhaps something significant couldn't be achieved after all, and so were anxious to reach the moon as soon as possible.

Despite all the treaties, Kennedy knew that the solar system might one day or another fall totally under the sphere of influence of one of the world's blocs. The first years—first months even—would be extremely important in this race into outer space. If the President, weakened by illness, gave up, if he left offce and handed the reins of power over to the Vice-President or to a political adversary, it might mean that he was yielding to Khrushchev a chance to establish space supremacy.

Like all tranquilizers, the pain-killer prescribed to Kennedy was a drug that reacted on the brain by disturbing its powers of reasoning. At the same time, it had the faculty of giving him the impression that he was extraordinarily lucid. Under the influence of this drug, the President of the United States felt that the possibility, however remote, of one bloc gaining control of the solar system constituted far more of a threat to humanity than the immediate danger of contagion from the JL3 virus. Doubtless his subconscious, in revolt against the pain his flesh was being made to endure, contributed to this warping of his reasoning powers. And his confidence that, given the chance, he would continue to succeed in his plans also played a role in his decision. If he took the JL3, he would be healthy, strong and indefatigable. And he would have about eleven months before he became contagious, eleven months to obtain an antidote from the Island laboratories.

When the overwheling pain returned, his hesitation vanished. He ordered his secretary not to disturb him for fifteen minutes, locked the doors of his office, opened the secret coffer and took out a small cardboard box closed by a rubber band. He took off the band, lifted up the cover, placed the box on his desk and sat down before it. He lifted a small piece of cotton and gazed at a tiny glass phial that contained a transparent liquid and rested on another bit of cotton.

Suddenly he realized that he didn't know how to take it, whether by mouth or as an injection. And if by injection, he didn't know whether it should be intravenous, intermuscular or subcutaneous.

Since he had no syringe, he decided to drink it. He broke open the phial at both ends, poured the contents into a glass, added a bit of water and drank. It was tasteless.

Not for a second did Kennedy think of immortality for himself, but only about acquiring the perfect health that would enable him to face up to his work.

He slipped the glass and all the other traces of the operation into a large kraft envelope and threw it down a closet incinerator used for certain records and other papers that had to be destroyed.

It is easy to imagine what it must have been like for Kennedy during the first hours of waiting for the virus to take effect. By the following day, his back pains had diminished, and at the end of a week, he felt completely rejuvenated. In the photographs taken of him during his last months, he seemed to bloom with vitality and youth. In the meantime, he had experienced the revealing symptom—he saw the color red in the night.

One of his doctors, persuaded that he was acting for the good of the nation and of Kennedy himself, sent regular reports on his visits to one of the Pentagon doctors, since the Pentagon had a section responsible for supervising the measures concerning the health and secruity of the President. The heads of state who knew the secret had three of their men stationed in this section. They were immediately informed of the sudden miraculous improvement in Kennedy's health. Another examination at the end of August confirmed that it was not an improvement but a cure. The cure was suspicious because it was medically impossible. Also, the Island's scientists had received two urgent messages from Kennedy asking that they accelerate their work on the antidote for the JL3. Finally, a servant at the White House informed a journalist, who had promised to publish nothing of what he learned, that the President had requested that all rugs, pictures and other objects containing the color red be taken out of his bedroom. The other heads of state knew then, beyond any doubt, that Kennedy had taken the JL3.

Still wearing his corset but rid of his pain and excited by his extraordinary renewal of energy, the President of the United States was delighted at having recovered his intellectual powers and the capacity for work demanded by the office he occupied and the man he was. But he was clear-sighted enough to understand just how enormous was the responsibility he had taken on his shoulders.

Even if the antidote were ready in time, even if it could be mass-produced quickly, it could not be given to the people without telling them the truth. And it was

clear that if they were told the truth, they would refuse
the antidote.

In drinking the contents of that phial, Kennedy had
transformed himself into a worldwide bombshell that
would explode in eleven months. He saw clearly the
only possible solution and immediately began to take the
necessary measures for grooming a successor.

He planned to turn over the reins of office to Vice-
President Johnson in June of 1964. Kennedy was sure
that, given his renewed mental and physical capacities,
he would have enough time before then to irrevocably
set in motion the different political initiatives he had in
mind. In agreement with Khrushchev and Mao, he
planned to announce in January, 1964, a reconciliation
of the United States with the Soviet Union and China. In
the spring, he planned to visit Moscow and Peking. And
in the course of this second voyage, the President's
plane would disappear at sea. The country would be
stirred by such deep emotion that Johnson's election in
November would be assured. Meanwhile, Kennedy
would be living on the Island.

He hoped he would be able to continue to direct
United States policies from the Island, or at least to influence them through Johnson, who would by then have
learned of the JL3 virus and the existence of Islet 307.
He was exalted by the idea of having all the time in the
world to influence humanity's future.

The vision of Kennedy, President of Immortality,
reappearing when the day had come to lead man toward
a future without limits in time and space, was a heady
one. It was not the dream of a paranoiac but a project
whose elements did have a basis in reality, and Kennedy
believed he was the man appointed by destiny to carry it
out.

He had already drafted his report for Johnson in case
of accident. He planned to write the last page on the day

he would leave for the Island, revealing to his successor the truth about his decision.

The other heads of state had made their joint decision. They could not allow any man, no matter who he might be, to let humanity run the risk of catching the virus. They didn't speak to each other of the possibility that Kennedy might find refuge on the Island, but they all had thought of it, and some considered that possibility just as dangerous as the threat of contamination.

It is here that "Mr. Smith" entered the picture once again. He was astonished only for a moment at the mission assigned to him. He didn't know who was paying him, and he received such conflicting information about it that he gave up trying to find out. He was of course pleased that the sum he would be receiving for the job would permit him to retire—and to disappear, which was prudent. He had made preparations for his retirement for some time. The heads of state were not certain the contagion would take a year to manifest itself, and Smith was therefore ordered to act with utmost speed. Mr. Smith knew men in all corners of the world who were ready and willing to carry out any assignment. He flew to the United States and began to set the stage. On the fifth of October, he returned to Rome to give a detailed account of his plan to his contact, an English official, son of a White Russian mother, anticapitalist and a sentimentally nostalgic Slav, who believed that he was acting under orders from a Soviet spy network.

On October 7, the heads of state conferred once again, and all but Adenauer accepted the plan. On the tenth, Adenauer resigned as Chancellor of the Reich and retired from political life. Mr. Smith received the green light on October 12 in Mexico. This time his contact was an American Army officer from Texas. But Mr. Smith, whose ear had tested all the accents in the world, detected an almost imperceptible trace of a Germanic accent in his speech. That same evening, Smith crossed the border into the United States.

On November 22, at 12:31 P.M. in Dallas, from a window on the sixth floor of the Texas School Book Depository, Lee Harvey Oswald shot one bullet into President Kennedy's neck. Another sniper, installed opposite the Depository, behind the railway embankment, fired in turn. Oswald fired a second shot, and the other marksman did likewise. Governor Connally was wounded. President Kennedy was dead.

Oswald was a dangerous, unstable mental case. He had been chosen only for his superior marksmanship. He was arrested by the police before there had been time to liquidate him. Jack Ruby was given the job of rectifying the error, and he killed Oswald two days later in the basement of the Dallas municipal police building. Ruby had been assured that he would have protection and immunity from prosecution. But he died in prison. Within four years, twenty-five people who had seen, heard or known something about the events at Dallas died of accidents, "suicide" or "heart attacks."

The results of the autopsy on Kennedy was never publicly revealed. His body was incinerated. His brain and his heart, which had been conserved, disappeared.

Chapter 29

On Wednesday, Ocotober 18, 1972, at seven o'clock in the evening, Dr. Lins, the gynecologist who had arrived from Sweden in 1956 and had delivered all the children born on the Island since, appeared on the television screens to propose a meeting. He usually looked twenty years younger than his sixty-two years, but now worry made him look his age. He asked all the doctors and biologists to meet with him two hours later in the round room to discuss an extremely important problem.

Such requests occurred frequently. The inhabitants of the Island often met in small or large groups, depending on the gravity of the problem or the number of specialists capable of giving their opinion about a particular question. But whatever the subject, the meetings were always open to everybody.

The meeting room, situated below the round garden, was in the same shape as the garden. A circular table with twenty-one seats occupied the center of the room, then two tiers of tables went around the first, reaching almost to the wall. Microphones had been placed everywhere, a camera installed on the ceiling and screens placed on the wall so that everyone could hear and see the person speaking.

The room was full. All seven of the Island's doctors, dressed in black overalls, were present. They spent their days doing research because they no longer had to deal with sick patients, and those rare individuals suffering from accidents recovered on their own after their wounds were dressed. There were 114 biologists, wearing blue overalls, and then other people, curious to know what the problem was, clad in various colors. All the seats were occupied, and many people stood leaning against the wall. Some children ran noiselessly among the tables. Others lay down on the tables and listened.

Roland sat next to Jeanne. The temperature of the room rose, and the breeze became a bit stronger, making the butterflies flutter about more than usual.

Dr. Lins spoke first.

"It has been ten years since I have served as an obstetrician, but I fear that very soon I shall be making up for that. I've been examining the girls for the past three days, and I think I can state that at least half of them between the ages of thirteen and eighteen are pregnant, which means one hundred to one hundred and twenty births are due next June."

The scientists present were horrified by the gravity of the situation.

"Are you certain of this?" Roland asked.

A girl's high-pitched voice interrupted him. She was a tall, slim redhead of fifteen or sixteen. Standing on a table, she jumped up and down excitedly, exclaiming, "And me, Doctor, am I pregnant?"

"What's your name?"

"Mary Ouspensky."

"Ouspensky, Mary, positive, you are pregnant," Lins replied.

Mary's green eyes became brilliant as emeralds, and she cried out, "Den, tell them. Tell them all that we're pregnant!"

Den, who was focusing the internal TV cameras on the meeting, pushed a button, and his voice announced everywhere on the Island the news that half the adolescent girls were pregnant.

Then he focused the cameras on Dr. Fuller, who had

just begun to speak. "This is a catastrophe. I feel I'm responsible. I shouldn't have warned them about fasting. My psychology was stupid."

"But how could you have foreseen such a result?" Galdos replied. "In the world outside, the women are afraid of becoming pregnant. For girls their age it's a curse, and for most of the older women it's a complication at the very least."

"But here on the Island, it's a disaster—for everyone, not only for those involved," Roland added.

"In any case," Galdos continued, addressing Fuller, "it's too late now. But it would have happened sooner or later. Most of them had already learned the trick of not eating meals from Annoa."

The word that came to all the adult minds was abortion. There was no other solution. They were all horror-stricken, looking at each other in consternation, the women even more disturbed than the men. The babies conceived during those three days in September were the grandchildren of everyone, even of those who had no children of their own, for they were the children of the Island where the collective body was as one. But there was no room for them.

Abortion as a collective act became a massacre, a butchery. The men and women fell silent, shrinking with loathing from the idea. Nobody dared pronounce the word.

Dr. Fuller said, "we might be able to keep several of them. There are a few places left."

Jeanne spoke up angrily. "You talk about them as though they were dogs. How many can we keep? How many will we drown? And how will they be chosen?"

Dr. Fuller flushed and replied, "I'd like to know if you have another solution to offer. If so, no one would be happier than I to adopt it."

"Very simple," Jeanne answered. "We could crowd together more, live two or three in a room."

"That's what we'll be forced to do when all the smaller children have grown," Roland said gently. "Most of the children live in the garden now. They'll want rooms as they grow up. Living space will become even scarcer than it is today."

Dr. Galdos rose and said, "It's absolutely not possible to consider the arrival of a new generation. We've already reached the extreme limit of our supportive capacity. If this new generation were to come into being, if we were to increase our level of density, which even today is barely tolerable, it would mean not only uncomfortable crowding but overwhelming congestion. We wouldn't be able to empty our waste products quickly enough, and in order to change our air, a permanent gust of wind would have to prevail on the Island. We would be at the mercy of a mechanical breakdown, of a twenty-four-hour delay in food deliveries. We would live under the perpetual threat of asphyxia, famine and poisoning. And all that would be nothing compared to the mental strain. There would no longer be, anywhere, for anyone, an instant of solitude, no living alone together for couples, no more silence, no more rest, no more meditation. Individuality would disappear. The inhabitants of the Island, and above all our children, would become immobile cells in a collective organism, each constantly, day and night, in contact with his neighbors. Nothing that goes to make up the personal character of a human being would be allowed to develop. It would mean an eternity of debasement or else a bloody revolt that would end with so many people dead that there would finally be plenty of room.

"And if we allow this first group of babies to be born, all the girls who are not yet pregnant will do everything possible to become so. They don't even need to fast but simply to eat only fruit, chocolate and all the other uncooked foods that we receive from the outside world, since only the cooked food prepared here contains the contraceptive. You can be sure that they know this already. And those who didn't know it before know it now that they've heard me. Afterward, we would have not just a hundred births in June but more by September. And if that amuses them, they will repeat the process, with each girl having two or three children. And their children might do the same.

"Excuse me for being so brutal. I'm doing it deliberately, to clear the air of all sentimentality. It's a question of survival. Not for each of us as individuals, which wouldn't be of any importance, but for the experiment we are making together, and that concerns all humanity. And more than humanity, all life in the universe.

"The fetuses must be prevented from becoming more than they are at this moment, almost abstract possibilities, without personality, without form, without consciousness. It can be done in forty-eight hours. We can't afford to wait one more day."

"You've seen the joy of the children," Jeanne replied. "They're pregnant because they wished to be. They want to have their babies. They won't agree to give them up."

"But they got pregnant just as they play marbles or billiards," Dr. Galdos answered. "It amused them. It was something new. They didn't understand the consequences. They aren't idiots. We'll explain the situation to them."

The worried men and women were silent. Some nodded their heads in agreement. Others expressed doubt.

"And it can't be allowed to happen again," Galdos continued. "We're men of science and have no fear of facts or words. We must immediately proceed to . . ."

But he was unable to pronounce that word he had pretended not to fear. He stuttered a little, perspired and finally found a paraphrase that made the image less intolerable.

"We must first neutralize the danger already situated

in the female factor, then render the masculine factor in-
offensive. We've behaved like idiots. We are living with
a powder keg, the female womb, along with an explosive
torch, the male penis, persuading ourselves that nothing
would happen if we kept the powder damp by mixing
contraceptives into the food. Well, it didn't work. I sug-
gest that we sterilize all the males on the Island, no matter what their age. The resectioning of the deferent
canals is a mild operation that leaves male virility intact.
We have few surgeons, but our biologists are used to
dissecting animals. And this important operation is a
simple and easy one, so I'm certain they could perform
it. Here is what we should propose to the people, so a
general decision can be made: suppression of the fertilized ovules, definitive neutralization of the male gonads.
The Island is a closed, airtight vessel from which no one
must leave but inside which new life must not come.
The content cannot become larger than the container. I
don't believe anyone will refuse to do what is necessary.
I myself will set the example and tomorrow will lie on
the operating table. I ask the women present to speak to
the pregnant girls. They will know better how to convince them than would the men. They are *our* daughters
after all, not morons, and will surely understand that it
would be stupid to give birth to babies only to have
them die, and to die with and because of them in ten or
twenty years."

Jeanne rose and spoke. "Having arrived so recently,
I'm not yet really assimiliated, and also I have personal
reasons for feeling myself to be slightly detached from
the rest of you. That may give me a more objective
point of view. It seems to me that we shouldn't be in
such a hurry. Some of you know that I wanted to experiment with the C41 antidote and did so. I've gone way
beyond the normal delay for catching the virus, which
seems to indicate that the C41 is effective. If this is true,

it means that one day we'll be able to envisage *leaving the Island*."

There was a general commotion. A yellow man said that much time would be needed to conclusively test the effectiveness of the C41. The present situation, however, was a pressing one. Each additional day would make the intervention more painful, distressing and difficult, both morally and physically.

Galdos pounded on the table: "Study, hopes, research, experiment, of course. But all that is for the future. So that the future can exist, the Island must be stabilized starting today."

A black man dressed in purple overalls rose. It was the Roman Catholic Bishop Davidson.

"What I have just heard has filled me with horror. I cannot support the measures proposed. You have sometimes committed the sacrilege of calling the Island 'paradise.' Now you want to make it a hell!"

The Bishop was suddenly replaced on the TV screens by Han's face as he called piteously for help.

Chapter 30

Annoa was stretched out on the grass in the garden, groaning and crying, bathed in the blue light of the Island night. Han stood beside her calling for help, his handsome face and golden hair illuminated by the TV camera's lights.

The animals were awakened by cries of suffering they had never heard before. Terrified, they fled in the night, colliding with tree trunks and bushes, while the birds smacked blindly against ceiling and walls. A Siamese cat leaped from branch to branch in a mad zigzag, and a fox raised its muzzle toward a nonexistent moon and began to howl.

From all corners of the Island, the boys and girls ran in the direction of the wails of pain, and the adults followed. Jeanne was among the first to arrive, and she immediately called for the light of day. The white light was turned on, changing night into day. The cat fell down onto the grass and stood with its tail vertically in the air, its back hairs bristling. The fox became quiet and the birds still.

Jeanne knelt beside Annoa and wiped her perspiring face. Taking her hand, she said in a reassuring voice, "Calm down, little one. Calm down. Lie back and relax. There. Good. Breathe the way I taught you to."

Annoa ceased moaning and looked at Jeanne questioningly.

"Yes," Jeanne said, smiling. "Yes, your baby is on its way."

The adults discreetly left.

Han had thought of nothing else for days, and now that the moment had arrived, it all seemed so extraordinary he couldn't believe it. He sank to his knees beside Annoa, repeating over and over again, "Annoa, Annoa. It's our baby being born!"

Annoa smiled at him lovingly, while the children ran and skipped about, then quietly formed a circle around them.

Another contraction made Annoa's face tighten in pain. Jeanne quickly told her to breathe in rhythm with the contractions. Annoa began to pant as Jeanne had taught her to do. All the children began to imitate Annoa as though they too were giving birth. Little by little the contractions stopped being painful, and at three in the morning, Jeanne said, "This is it, darling. The head is beginning to come out. It's blond like its father."

The boys and girls gathered around Annoa to see the infant leave her body. A boy fainted. Han trembled. Jeanne took the baby and lifted it up so Annoa could see its face and its sex.

Annoa murmured in an exhausted voice, "It's a girl!"

Tears of happiness ran down her face. Jeanne shook the infant and tapped its back to make it cry out and open up its lungs. As the baby screamed, Jeanne placed it on Annoa's belly.

Chapter 31

When President Nixon went to Peking in February, 1972, people thought a new era in history was beginning. Communist Asia and the capitalist West seemed to be in a conciliatory mood and bent on coordinating their efforts toward peace.

But the truth lay elsewhere. Nixon's voyage had two secret aims, of which the first was known only to Brezhnev and Queen Elizabeth and the second to himself alone.

First, and this secret he could not confide even to Kissinger, he wanted to find out if Mao had taken the JL3 virus. Mao's superb health, his "long swim" in the Yangtze River at an age when most men are just about able to tolerate a footbath, his disappearances from public view followed by ever-healthier-looking reappearances, had disturbed those heads of state sharing the secret. De Gaulle was the first of them to wonder whether China's leader had not followed in Kennedy's footsteps. If he had, he had certainly taken precautions against infecting his people, since China was so concerned with keeping its population down to avoid the terrible famine that threatened at every turn. If that were the case, his biologists must have found a means to prevent the virus from spreading. Nixon was determined to find out the truth.

De Gaulle had officially recognized China, and Mao was discreetly informed that the French President would not refuse an invitation to Peking. De Gaulle was sure that if he met with the Chinese leader, he would be able to discern whether Mao had taken the virus or not. But he was not invited. After he had retired to Colombey, and right before he died, de Gaulle told Nixon, Brezhnev and Elizabeth about his suspicions regarding Mao.

After de Gaulle's death, Nixon took the burden on his shoulders. Two years later, he succeeded in opening the way to Peking. But by that time, another perhaps more terrifying problem had come to his attention. Reports of the intelligence services and photographs transmitted by the Pentagon satellite above Chinese territory revealed that China was preparing something of momentous importance.

To the southeast of Nanchang, a huge region one quarter the size of Texas was being completely transformed. Thousands of workers were building runways, rail lines, outside hangars, canals, underground passages and storage pits. The Pentagon had immediately concluded that the site was being prepared as a vast shooting range for intercontinental rockets intended for use against America or Russia or both. Therefore, fifty-eight nuclear missiles had been turned away from their first objective and aimed toward that area.

Nixon had approved the Pentagon action. But he had an even greater fear of what China might be planning.

At the very moment when the United States was phasing down the Apollo program and the Soviet Union was slowing down its Luna program, he suspected that China might be preparing a gigantic space surprise. It was very strange that China, at least until now, had made no effort in that direction and had manifested no curiosity about the planets. The rapidity with which it had constructed atomic and hydrogen bombs proved that it was not lack of technical know-how that was holding them up. And cost was of no consequence in the People's Republic of China.

In his study of Chinese history, Nixon had learned that the Chinese had been the first astronomers, even before the Chaldeans and thousands of years before the Europeans. They had also been the first to invent rockets, the first to explore the deep mysteries of the earth with their seismographs, the first to understand the energy lines of the acupuncture medians that even now perplex Western physiologists.

It was impossible that with such a past China should be disinterested in the space race. It was much more probable that, with all its power and isolation, China was in the process of preparing a fantastic departure into space that would leave the Soviet and American cosmonauts far behind. The dimensions of the preparations detected by the satellite were beyond belief. But then, so were the stakes. Although the U.S. and the U.S.S.R. had been synchronizing their space efforts ever since the meeting between Krushchev and Kennedy in Vienna, the Soviet and American leaders knew that one day history would decide whether the solar system was to be communist or capitalist, depending on which bloc proved to be strongest or cleverest at the right moment. However, once he had seen the photographs of the area south of Nanchang, Nixon wondered if the option might not have changed, becoming a question of whether the solar system would be dominated by the Chinese.

As a good American laywer, he had decided to ask Mao direct questions concerning space and the JL3 virus. He had studied Chinese for two years and knew enough of the language to pronounce several precise phrases and to understand "yes" or "no." Moreover, he was aware that Mao spoke a little English, since they had on several occasions talked to each other on their private telephone line when rendered necessary by events concerning the Island.

But Nixon wasn't alone with Mao for a single minute during his historic visit to China. The continual presence of a Chinese interpreter—insisted upon by Mao himself —made it impossible for Nixon to mention the JL3. He also couldn't mention the Nanchang project, because that would have caused Mao to lose face by forcing him to acknowledge before a third party that his territory was being spied upon, which he very well knew anyway.

However, Nixon did find the occasion to say to him, as a joke, "I've been wondering if you ever see red at night."

Mao grinned from ear to ear and spoke a few words that the interpreter translated proudly: "China is ever red, day as well as night!"

When the President of the United States returned to his country, he knew no more than when he had left it. The work going on south of Nanchang could have several interpretations. It might be the preparation for the greatest space experiment ever known, or perhaps it was only the infrastructure for the industrialization of a new region or for a new system of irrigation.

As to Mao's health, it had seemed to Nixon too good to be normal. But then, it might be that tomorrow one would learn of his sudden death. There was no proof either way.

Nixon decided to discuss it with Brezhnev. Capitalist-Marxist antagonism must disappear before the possibility of Chinese settlement of the planets and the transformation of the solar system into a yellow beehive. White solidarity must prevail.

On his return to Washington, Nixon telephoned Brezhnev, and three months later he was in Moscow.

Chapter 32

Jeanne had done everything possible for Annoa and the new-born infant. Han lay down next to Annoa and held her to him, with the child placed in the valley formed by their two bodies curled up against each other. All three fell quickly and happily asleep.

Jeanne had trouble convincing herself that the infant wouldn't catch cold, that no microbe could attack it, that it was safer than a day-old lamb or an hour-old kitten. It belonged to a new human species that had no need for protection against outside aggression. It was as healthy and natural as if it had been born to Adam and Eve in the Garden of Eden. Jeanne lay down beside them and slept as they did.

The white light slowly faded. All the children slept too, as tired out as Annoa by the birth of the baby girl to whom she had given the name Hannao, a combination of Han's name and her own.

Daylight returned on schedule. When Jeanne opened her eyes, Roland was standing beside her, smiling. He held out his hands and pulled her toward him. He was going to clasp her in his arms and she was going to let him do it, when suddenly she realized that she must be exceedingly unattractive at such an early hour. She turned and ran to a brook, knelt down, plunged her face in the water and ran her fingers through her short hair, before returning to Roland with a smile on her face. She hadn't been back to her room and so hadn't taken any tranquilizers. Strangely enough, she felt better for it. Perhaps having slept outside on the grass, or washed in the brook or helped bring a child into the world had caused this euphoria.

She took Roland's arm as they watched Annoa nursing her baby at the foot of a linden tree. Han arrived with food and flowers. The boys and girls who were not still sleeping clustered around Annoa with delight. The Siamese cat ran around chasing a sleepy blackbird that was looking for worms. The flowers gave forth exotic perfumes, making the air redolent with heady scent. Jeanne suddenly felt extraordinarily happy.

"They don't need you any longer," Roland said. "Come on."

They ate a real French breakfast of hot croissants and coffee with milk on the beach, and Roland told her of the latest development.

"Some biologists, Dr. Lins and I are going to meet with Bahanba. I would like you to come along too. In a way, it will be the end of the meeting that was interrupted by Han last night when Annoa began her labor pains. We need Ba's advice."

"Is he still capable of giving advice?"

"He can barely speak, but he's approaching total wisdom through serenity of mind."

Chapter 33

Bahanba's mind and spirit floated on a sea of utter
tranquility. A glass of water taken daily was all that he
had consumed for five weeks. He felt his flesh slowly
dissolving. Finally liberated by his fast from all affective
ties to his own body, he looked upon it only as the bal-
last anchoring his spirit to the earth. His weight was
diminishing by the hour; he had become like a dry leaf
and would soon weigh nothing.

As he neared the moment when he would be delivered from his mortal flesh, Bahanba felt a detached
affection for it. His mind finally perceived and understood his body's internal mechanisms: from the great
work of its organs to the endless tasks of its cells. The
body, a purifying instrument, was the great work of creation by the Supreme Universal Spirit, God, God had
made the body in order to allow the soul in transition to
become cleansed and worthy of communion with God.
Bahanba wondered if his soul had reached that state of
ideal purity and harmony, or whether he must still trav-
erse a thousand times a thousand lives before becoming
One with the Supreme Universal Spirit.

Galdos explained the situation to Bahanba. Also
standing beside Bahanba's bed were many of the Island's scientists, including Roland and Jeanne. Way in
the back, behind all the others, stood Samuel Frend.

Bahanba lay immobile, his eyes closed, his respiratory
movements barely visible. The skin on his face was

stretched so tightly over the bones that his features resembled those of a three-thousand-year-old mummy.
But life still glowed behind the wasted mask.

While he was meditating, Bahanba listened. He was
beyond pain and sorrow, fast reaching that plateau
where All melted into One.

When Galdos had finished speaking, Bahanba's chest
heaved slightly. He saw clearly what would happen if
something were done and what would happen if nothing
were done. One or the other eventuality was a tiny unimportant event, but perhaps a necessary one, in the
eternal scheme of Being. Although they would not understand, he must try to tell them. His lips opened and they
heard him whisper: "The world moves, the Island moves,
paradise is immobile. What happens is not what is. Do
something or do nothing. Truth is all."

He fell silent, and his breathing once more became
imperceptible.

Silently his visitors left. When they were in the street,
Galdos spoke again. "Did you understand? I didn't. He's
beginning to make no sense. We have to make a decision without him, and instantly. The Island moves, yes,
that's for sure, it's begun to move too much! And we
have to put a stop to it. There's the truth. I'm going to
ask the adults to vote for or against the abortion and vas-
ectomy plans. Then we'll ask the girls to see the doctors
and biologists. Everything must be decided today. Don't
you agree with me?"

Jeanne couldn't think of any way to refute Galdos.
She clung close to Roland and shivered. He comforted
her gently.

"It seems monstrous to us because there are so many
of them, but for each individually it won't be so bad.
And the fetuses have not yet developed enough to be
considered as anything more than ovules without feeling."

Galdos launched an appeal over the TV sets again for

those who might have missed the previous day's discussions, repeating everything, asking the adults to think over the problem and requesting all those who did not agree with his proposal to notify Dr. Lins before evening. Afterward, the children would finally be asked for their opinion, since the matter concerned them all.

By evening, none of the adults had said they were opposed. But the children had not waited to express their opinion. All day long they had joyously shouted and sung their desire not only to keep the babies already conceived but to conceive others as well. None of them ate any food prepared on the Island, and they made love constantly. All the children visited Annoa and Han during the day to see the newborn infant, amazed at how tiny and beautifully formed it was. And when evening fell, the boys and girls had almost forgotten what Galdos had asked, because the whole idea seemed to them so false, so unbelievable, so unimportant.

The doctors and biologists met once again in Galdos's room. Jeanne began to talk, wanting to convince them, and perhaps herself as well, that there was a way out of the predicament.

"We now know that the girls won't go to the doctors out of their own free will. Are we going to force them to do so, and if so, how? Are we going to be obliged to disavow the Island's ideal of liberty? Are we adults going to play the role of policemen?"

She looked around at the others. Frend was seated in a corner, as far away from her as he could get. She looked straight at him and for a moment had a curious feeling of recognition. She wanted to catch his eye but, as she continued to speak, she automatically turned toward the other faces in the room.

"Since the C41 antidote seems to be working, couldn't we experiment more and perhaps open up the Island sometime in the not too distant future? Maybe it will be possible to do that in less than twenty years. And

we can let the third generation come into the world,
looking upon it as a difficulty rather than a disaster."

They listened in silence. Jeanne was proof of a possible but unsubstantiated solution, a solution still worthy
of consideration despite the danger. It was a slight hope,
not by any means a certainty, but they were exhausted
from worry and had lost the habit of dealing with pressing problems and torments. Also, they wanted desper-
ately to share in the children's joy, even though they
knew how irresponsible it was.

"Well," replied Galdos, "I don't see what else we can
do. We need more technicians. We should send for them
immediately and put them to work on the C41. In three
months, we'll know where we are."

Dr. Lins sighed and said, "I hope to God you're right,
Jeanne."

They seperated in a kind of artificial euphoria that
masked the anguish they all felt. For once, they were
trusting in feeling and not in reason. There would be
time enough to think it over clearly tomorrow.

Roland asked Jeanne to dine in his room and cele-
brate with him this day that might have ended in sadness
but had instead become a day of hope.

Silently, Jeanne took his arm. They passed through
the garden, where many of the children were sleeping
and others were still singing. Near the brook, they found
Han and Annoa seated on the grass close to a fire, their
baby asleep between them. Den was humming a song,
and Mary lay next to him, wondering if he were the
father of the child she was carrying. Roland picked an
armful of roses and when they returned together in his
room, he placed them in a vase before the television
screen, which he cut off so they wouldn't be disturbed.
He didn't want to know anything about the Island or the
world this evening. The roses were in full bloom, red as
blood and joy.

Jeanne ordered extravagantly over the phone: requesting a frying pan, lettuce, oil, fresh eggs, tarragon, cream, truffles, strawberries and champagne. She laughed until she cried when five minutes later the automatic wagon arrived with everything she had asked for. She prepared a magnificent light omelet, just as she used to do at the rue de Vaugirard. They drank to the happiness of others and then to themselves. Jeanne was relaxed, almost joyous. For one evening, she wanted to believe she was still the Jeanne of earlier days and that she hadn't changed any more than had Roland. It was a gala evening, slightly mad, truly marvelous. For this night, she turned her back on tomorrow. Tomorrow would come, of course, but tonight she wished to forget everything. Tomorrow there would be time enough to think of the cares of the Island, and about taking tranquilizers again to calm her spirit. And the day after tomorrow would be a little less difficult, and the day after that easier still. She would live for each day in itself. Tonight was unique, a night from the past on the rue de Vaugirard, with Roland beside her, the same Roland as in those bygone years. Speaking in the same low, warm voice, he repeated their old words of tenderness and desire. The Island no longer existed.

Then came the moment she feared but had been waiting for during a third of her life. Roland turned out the lights, and she basked in the black protection of the night that might enable Roland to forget the Jeanne of today and remember only his Jeanne of their happy past. She had decided that they would have this night, and then she would part from him, little by little, heartened by this last stolen moment of happiness, on her voyage toward the tranquillity of old age.

He took her in his arms and kissed her tenderly, then more and more passionately, and it was once again as it had been in their most perfect moments of love on the rue de Vaugirard. Jeanne closed her eyes to hide her tears of mixed pleasure and distress. When she opened them, she received a shock that made her recoil in horror. She saw flames of red everywhere!

She understood immediately and cried out, "Roland, Roland, *I can see the roses in the dark!*" She tore herself from his arms crying, "It's horrible."

She wasn't thinking of what the failure of the C41 meant for the Island, only of the horrible image of herself twenty years older than Roland for eternity.

Caught in a trap like a wild beast, she threw on her clothes and ran out into the street. The streets were blue in the night, but there were other red objects she had never noticed before. The shortest way to her room was through the garden. There, she saw the groups of sleeping children strewn about like brilliant bouquets of flowers. She stood paralyzed at the sight of all those magnificent girls who would one day be eighteen and remain that age, perhaps giving birth to daughters who would remain young like them. And Roland would be livng among those lovely young things, Roland a man of just over thirty years surrounded by adolescents, a man rare and hard as a diamond. While she, Jeanne, would remain an example of another era when the flesh had changed along with the spirit, a specimen conserved by the JL3 as if by formaldehyde, indestructibly the same, always and forever twenty years older than Roland, those damned years when she had burnt herself out searching for him.

Suddenly, she remembered the kidnapping attempts in Paris and London. The first time they had wanted to take her because they thought she was contaminated, but the second time it had been Roland who had asked that she be brought to him on the Island along with his children. He had never mentioned it in order to avoid causing her even more terrible pain and regret. He had never even spoken of his children's arrival, so that she wouldn't realize what he had tried to do and what she had missed by not giving in. If she had let them take her, today she would be young! She had been stupid and obstinate, she had killed only to deny herself eternal youth and happiness. She gasped in horror and continued to run.

At the door of the garden, she ran blindly into a man in black who excused himself. She recognized Dr. Lins and cried out, "It's over! The C41 has failed. I can see red in the night. I'm contaminated and the virus has won. I'm lost forever!"

Chapter 34

Dr. Lins was the only gynecologist on the Island. With each passing year, his work had increasingly inspired him with great tenderness, pity and admiration for women and the marvelous mysteries of their bodies. He felt an infinite compassion for the young girls on the Island who, obeying the demands of their bodies, showed themselves to be more womanly than their mothers, become more pragmatic with age and less concerned with the joys their bodies could offer. Through these young girls, life was going to continue.

As he watched them sleeping in the garden, Dr. Lins was distressed for them as though they were his own daughters. He had hoped with all his heart that the decision taken at the evening meeting was not just a delay but a door opening on the future.

Jeanne's words closed that door irrevocably. He cast a final glance toward the garden full of flowers and children. Two steps away from him, a boy and girl were sleeping in each other's arms, and he thought he recognized the girl. She was one of the youngest of those pregnant, only fourteen, innocent and beautiful. He sighed and walked away, his head bent and shoulders drooping.

Life continues, spreads, spills over, without taking circumstances into account. Here, by continuing to multiply, it was going to end by bringing about its own destruction. Yes, it was necessary to make the girls abort. Because he was a gynecologist, the word didn't frighten him. It was after all only a technical word. What horrified him was the surgical act itself. He had done only one abortion and that on a pregnant woman who would have died had she given birth. Here all the mothers were in danger of dying and all the others in the community with them.

Action had to be taken immediately. They could no longer waste time discussing the problem. Each day that passed would make the operation more painful.

But what operation?

Dr. Lins was the only person to ask himself that question—how? It was easy to say that over a hundred young girls must have abortions. It was less easy to do it, especially when the girls were so determined to have their babies.

Chapter 35

In the middle of the night, Samuel Frend got up to drink a glass of water. An hour later, he was awakened by a sharp pain in his stomach followed by acute nausea. He vomited, rinsed out his mouth and took an aspirin with another glass of water. The pain and nausea disappeared. This had never happened to him before. He wondered if someone had discovered who he really was and was trying to poison him, and if so, with what. He fell asleep trying to remember whom he had been with the day before, in order in pinpoint when and how the poison could have been administered to him.

He was awakened again by new pains. As he opened his eyes, his TV screen lit up and bells rang, signaling a general alarm. He ran to the bathroom as a man appeared on the screen dressed in the red overalls of the chemists. Frend had met him but didn't remember his name.

While vomiting again over the sink, he heard the man's voice shouting, "Don't drink the water. It's poisoned. Don't drink from the faucets, fountains or brooks. Don't drink any water!"

The warning signal rang again, and this time the chemist addressed the children in the garden, asking them to awaken those who were still asleep. Then he rapidly explained what had happened. The several children and adults who had drunk water during the night had become violently nauseous and had vomited like Frend. But the chemist, who had suffered the same symptoms, had reacted as a chemist. He had set about at once trying to locate the toxin that had upset him. He had begun by analyzing the water from his faucet and found that it contained a foreign substance.

"I don't know what poison is in the water. I haven't had time to do a thorough analysis. But I can tell you that the water should remain clear and colorless when certain reagents are placed in it, and instead our water becomes clouded and turns light yellow. I don't think the poison is dangerous because, if it were, I would not be here speaking to you about it. But it has a very nasty effect, as those of you who have taken it can testify. I'm going to take water from the central reservoir and analyze it, because all of the Island's water is undoubtedly contaminated. Don't drink any at all! I don't know how this could have happened. In any case, and now I'm speaking to the technicians, we must close the reservoir and branch the waterworks for fresh water directly into the pump room. The distribution will be irregular, but in a few hours, we'll be able to drink at least a small amount of water while the reservoir is being emptied and disinfected. The other chemists and myself will—"

An anxious voice cut in. "Please, let me speak. I have something to say regarding the water. I know what has happened. Let me tell you."

The chemist's astonished face disappeared from the screens, and Dr. Lin's image appeared. "I poisoned the water," he said.

Frend had returned to bed. His stomach spasms were diminishing in intensity and frequency. He wiped the perspiration from his forehead.

Lins continued, "I had hoped, given the early hour of the morning, that everyone, or at least the people for whom this product was intended, would have absorbed it before someone would discover that it had been transported by the water. I am deeply sorry that the alarm has been given.

"Rest assured that this product is not toxic when diluted in great quantities of water. It simply provokes contractions of the diaphragm, and, among women, contractions of the uterus sufficient to expulse a fertilized egg. Yes, I did it to cause the pregnant girls to abort. Because our hope has been an illusion and is now dead. There is no antidote to the contagion of immortality. The C41 has failed. Madame Jeanne Corbet became infected with the JL3 virus during the night. She is going to tell you about it herself. Madame Corbet, wherever you are, do you hear me, and will you confirm this?"

There was an eerie silence. While Lins waited, his face became distorted with pain and fear.

"Madame Corbet, I beg of you, this is very grave. Would you please repeat before everyone what you told me about last night, that you are contaminated and see red in the dark."

Jeanne's pale face and staring eyes flashed on the screen. She resembled a ghost and spoke in a voice barely above a whisper. "It's true."

Roland's voice burst out over the microphones: "Jeanne, where are you? Jeanne, I'm looking for you!"

Jeanne's image left the TV screens.

In the garden, beside the brook, Mary was stretched out on the grass, writhing and twisting in agony, holding her belly. She had awakened an hour before and drunk some water.

"I have assumed my responsibilities as a doctor," Dr. Lins said. "This was the only way to force the girls to stop their pregnancies. And it's still possible. I ask that the reservoir not be emptied. I ask the technicians not to branch the waterworks onto the pumps.

"It will take eleven days to entirely renew the water in the reservoir. Nobody can go that long without drinking. I ask the adults to guard the reservoir and the waterworks. We must drink this water to save ourselves and the Island. We're all going to suffer together. The women will suffer more than the men and the pregnant girls more than the others. But when this is all over, the Island will no longer be in danger. I ask forgiveness from those who are going to lose the infant they wanted to keep."

Davidson, the black Bishop, jumped up from his bed and began to lash out verbally at the screen. "Hypocrite. Murderer. Sadist! God should twist your guts around your neck!"

Davidson fell to his knees and begged God's pardon for himself, for the children, for all those who knew not what they did. He began to weep, then went to the sink and drank two glasses of water.

Samuel Frend's mission did not include interference in events on the Island, but it now seemed imperative to do something about this crisis. He dressed, took a pack of cigarettes and a pen from his closet, made a wry face as his stomach rebelled again at the water he had swallowed and ran toward the waterworks. Other adults, convinced by Dr. Lins, hastened in the same direction. Frend knew the waterworks inside out, as well as all the operations for conversion of saltwater into freshwater. When he arrived at the immense blue gallery, a violent battle was going on between some adults and a group of adolescent boys and girls trying to reach the controls of the valves connecting the waterworks to the pump room. It wasn't exactly a battle since no one was armed; the adults were merely trying to make a barrier and to push back their assailants. Their fighting position was weak since they didn't dare hurt their sons and daughters. The latter were wildly furious. They scratched and bit, and at last one of them seized a monkey wrench hanging on the wall and hit out with it. Somebody's face was cut open and the blood poured out. Other girls and boys seized upon any instrument they could find and in several minutes had forged an opening toward the valves.

At the other end of the hall, Frend tore open his pack of cigarettes and crushed the contents. This was the plastic explosive. He put it in the place he had spotted and screwed his pen into it, after having regulated a tiny mechanism, the detonator.

He saw other adults and young people arriving and noted that the battle was becoming more intense near the valves. He left rapidly by way of a ladder that led to a trapdoor in the ceiling. The explosion occurred just as he stepped outside, shaking the ground under his feet. He had just put out of commission the pump that brought the seawater into the waterworks for conversion into freshwater.

He grabbed at the first microphone he could find and said, "Stop fighting. It's useless. The pump bringing the seawater into the waterworks has just blown up. It will take at least a week to repair it or get another pump. There's only the water in the reservoir. We must drink it, to save the Island."

A group of young people came running. Frend raced to his room.

Roland looked everywhere for Jeanne. She wasn't in her room, and no one had seen her after her appearance on the screen. He returned again to the garden, where he was rudely pushed aside by a group of young children leaving it. They began to hit him with their fists, and a girl bit his right hand. He cried out with surprise and pain, broke away and slapped her. The girl screamed, the boys threw Roland to the ground and kicked him. A blow across his throat took his breath away. He had the impression that he was being stampeded by sheep. He threw his arm back, striking several of them in the legs and making them fall. Finally, he got up, pushed the others aside and forced his way into the garden.

Once inside, he realized that it wasn't possible to go any farther. The children were like bees in a hive that has just been overturned. And there was the same sort of sharp, enraged, menacing, collective hum.

Surrounded by frightened children, Mary lay beside the brook, moaning and weeping. Den knelt beside her, trying to calm her. He took her under the arms and helped her to get up. He thought she might feel less pain if she walked. When she was upright, several drops of blood ran down her legs. Den laid her down again, raised his arms, clenched his fists and shouted out in a frenzy of fury.

It was seven in the morning on Islet 307, and the white light of day shone in the Citadel. Outside the Island, on the ocean, it was still night, a black night thickened by a heavy fog in which Admiral Kemplin's ships turned round and round like blind bats, using their radar to feel out the location of the other vessels and sounding their warning sirens. In his cabin on the aircraft carrier, the Admiral was furious. He had just drunk some abominable powdered coffee that was too hot and had burnt his tongue. The night had been long and day would be extremely short, swallowed up in a peasoup fog. He thought they would be lucky if five or six hours went by without a collision. Also, he was becoming unnerved by the "idiot Russians" with their "trawlers" and the "vermin Chinese" with their "junks," who came perilously near the American ships, as though they wanted to cause a nasty incident that would make trouble for him. While he shaved nervously with his electric razor, he reminded himself that he would be leaving the following week. He pitied his replacement. He planned to take two months' leave, go to Florida, and bask in the sun, far from the fog and this unearthly sea and sky. He smiled happily.

Chapter 36

Once in his own room, Frend barricaded his door, opened his closet, removed the camouflage from his installation. Next, he made sure everything was in good working order. He pushed the buttons on the TV screen to receive views of the different locations on the Island screened by the cameras. He saw the blue gallery of the waterworks emptying and the adults carrying away their wounded and dead. He saw the garden in an uproar, filled with a mass of children grouped around Han and Den.

Frend had been instructed to set up certain installations there, which he had done, and to inform the three remaining heads of state aware of the secret if a grave crisis were to occur. He was now going to do that. He had decided not to tell them what he had done to the waterworks. Even the most loyal of agents tells his superiors only what he deems it wise to reveal.

He pulled out the case from its hiding-place and began to tap out a message in Morse code, using the yellow button.

At the White House in Washington, President Nixon had just ended a conference with two agricultural advisers. A secretary brought him a handwritten message. Smiling, Nixon thanked the two men for their recommendations. They left, and he told the secretary he wished to remain alone and undisturbed in his office.

In Moscow, it was night, and Brezhnev was leaving the Kremlin in his large black limousine when the tele-

phone rang. He listened to the voice at the other end
and ordered the chauffeur to return to the Kremlin.

In Peking, the head of the monitoring service was
awakened in the middle of the night by the radioman on
duty, and he in turn awoke Chairman Mao.

Chapter 37

"Never, never, never," cried the young girl, "never,
never, never!"

That meant "I shall never give up my child, never
drink this water that will destroy it, never bow before
the decision taken by the adults, never try to understand
their reasons!"

Now all the children were assembled in the garden.
The smaller children of ten and twelve, for whom the
problem of pregnancy was really of no importance, cried
out in unison with their older brothers and sisters. For
them it was like a game. The pregnant girls, or those
who thought they might be, beat against the invisible
wall closing in on them. They didn't want to obey and
knew they might be forced to do so.

They were beginning to feel thirsty, not real thirst yet,
but the obsession of wanting to drink the fresh water
they saw in the middle of the grass and the bowers. The
boys began to feel something new, something never experienced before, in their muscles, their throats, their
blood—the need to run, to yell, to hit, to break, to destroy. It was the seething birth of the instincts of migra-
tion and violence.

"We should kill them all!" screamed a dark, curly-haired boy.

Han shouted back, "Where will that get us?"

Standing beside a large bush covered with thousands of blue flowers, he held his infant daughter in his arms, while Annoa clung to him. He spoke calmly to all those who were listening. "Even if they were all dead, we'd still be left with only the water of the reservoir that we'd be forced to drink."

"But what can we do, then?" a girl cried out.

"We must leave," Han said, and his voice rose with exaltation. "There'll be room for all of us in the closed boats and rubber crafts that haven't been burned. If we stay here, we'll lose our children. We must leave the Island."

A cry of joy and approval answered him. Then some worried voices cried, "They'll shoot us!"

"The warships are out there."

"They'll destroy us."

"If we pass beyond the buoys, they'll shell us."

Shoot, shell, destroy—they had seen all that a thousand times on the television screens, but they had also seen unlimited space, planes flying in an endless blue sky, the Apollo rocket shooting up into space without end, and the streets of New York, Paris and other great cities with their masses of cars and their skyscrapers reaching toward the skies, real skies without a ceiling, outside the walls, outside, outside!

"We've never tried to cross the second line of buoys," Han replied. "They won't dare fire on us. We'll tell them we're naked children, and they won't fire. We must leave immediately."

The boys and girls began to run toward the garden gates.

They saw Dr. Galdos's horrified image on the television screens as he addressed them. But they paid no attention. He begged them not to leave, explained that they would be killed, but the children believed only that their departure would lead them to the fabulous world outside.

Chapter 38

Jeanne knelt at Bahanba's bedside. She told the dying man, who now weighed almost nothing but whose spirit seemed to fill the room with a glow, about her search for Roland, her endless battles, her hopes, her despair on arriving at the Island, her resignation, then her revolt when she had seen the red roses in the night. And when she finished her story, she continued to talk, complaining like a tired, beaten child, pouring out all her torments in an effort to escape from the terrible solitary silence that had imprisoned her in a corset of iron for fifteen years. The words she spoke were a poison emptying out of her, a world of parasites eating her up, that she was now purging from her system.

When the eleven white boats, swaying in the breeze, were full and sitting in close order along the small circular pier, half of the children were still left on the shore. Den, who was among them, cried: "Let's go and get the rafts!"

There were seven flat-bottomed rubber rafts and he knew where they were. He didn't know how to inflate them but was sure he would figure out a way of doing so. All the remaining children followed Den to the wharf where the rafts were located.

The four armed men guarding the exit from the channel had argued and protested to prevent the youngsters from climbing into the boats, but they hadn't fired on them. They couldn't shoot their own children.

Alone with Annoa and their two-day-old daughter, Han was in the smallest boat, a barge different from the others and resembling a Chinese junk. The ten larger boats were filled to overflowing.

The four guards, who had not been able to stop the youngsters, locked the transparent, airtight covers over the boats, since those who went out in the boats must not be able to open them when outside the limits of the Citadel. The children let them do it because they were accustomed to that procedure, not realizing that it made them virtual prisoners inside the small craft. The electric motors hummed, and the hermetically sealed white boats passed one after the other into the special flooding chamber, received the rain of acid and sailed out onto the open sea.

Jeanne fell silent. After purging herself of all her memories and sufferings, they came flooding back in their entirety, intact with the knowledge that nothing could ever change, that she would be twenty years older than Roland for eternity.

She got up slowly, looked at Bahanba and whispered, "What can I do?"

Bahanba said nothing. He was like a dead god, the supreme form of life. He had heard and understood everything, but he no longer spoke aloud. The answer could be found only in his silence. Jeanne listened, waited and received no message. At a loss, she looked anxiously at the face now reduced to its basic bone structure, at the closed eyes looking inward toward another vision, and she saw nothing and understood nothing. Bahanba was now only spirit and mind, while Jeanne was flesh and blood. She left the room.

Frend watched the television screen while he simultaneously informed the three heads of state of what was happening on the Island. Each of the three leaders was alone in his office, where an orderly brought in a letter-by-letter transcription of the messages received in Morse code.

Frend sent the messages uncoded because of the time limitation. But the services that picked up his words believed they were a code and looked vainly for the sense in phrases like "Naked children have left in sealed boats."

The messages were transmitted in English, which Brezhnev and Mao understood perfectly well. Each chief of state had his hot line near at hand as well as the small case Frend had brought each of them.

On the Island, leaning over the drinking trough in the round stable, the white buffalo drank his fill.

As soon as they left the channel, the boats sailed into night and fog. They had neither compass nor other navigational aids. Their instrument boards included only a sending and receiving radio set and a single dial-face on which a mobile luminous arrow indicated the direction of the Island and the entrance to the channel. These boats were not intended for sailing on the open sea. Rather they were meant always to return to the Island.

Surrounded by fog, each boat lost sight of the others. Han's boat was the last. Standing at the wheel, hemmed in by the gray obscurity and the rain pouring down on the transparent roof, Han was calm and self-assured. His instinct, as sure as that of a bird, told him exactly in which direction he would find the free sky and sun he was seeking. He turned left, sailing slowly toward the south.

The sound of the alarm could be heard everywhere.

Admiral Kemplin leaped toward the bridge of the aircraft carrier. The man in charge of the radar yelled out his information. "Eleven unidentified objects have left the Island, ten large and one small. The large ones are heading due west toward the buoys. The small one is turning south."

Suddenly, the Admiral gave the orders. "Helicopters aloft. Follow by radar the eleven objects. Fly overhead. Prepare to drop napalm.

"Planes aloft—circle above the objectives.

"Planes ready to take off—do so immediately.

"Ships in the first, second and third rows—prepare the flamethrower batteries."

The first boat sailing due west crossed the first line of buoys. A naked girl was at the wheel.

The black of the night and the heavy mist hid the buoys. The girl continued to steer westward. Suddenly, the night turned red with lights, and a voice cried out from the radio receiver inside the boat, "Return, go back. Return or we'll annihilate you. Turn back or you'll be destroyed!"

The terrified children left their benches and shouted back, "We're naked children. We're the children from the Island. Let us pass!"

Five other boats had joined the first. They crossed the second line of buoys, spreading out in a fan of less than two hundred yards.

"We're the children from the Island. Let us pass!"

The other boats came up behind them, and in the transmitters of all ten boats, ten voices repeated the same phrase with the same certitude of being heard and understood. They were the voices of children to whom no one had ever done any harm.

On the radar screens, the ten boats comprised a small flotilla sailing in almost perfect order, speeding on its way toward the west. The pilots in the aircraft and ships, the flamethrowers and napalm bombers, heard the concert of youthful voices saying, "We're children, children from the Island. Let us pass."

Then they heard the Admiral's cold, steady voice. "Open fire!"

Cutting through the thick mist, rivers of flames poured forth and exploded on, around and under the boats. In the process, the plastic melted and burned, causing green explosions. The men in the aircraft and on the ships heard screams of pain and terror in their earphones, and then nothing. The camera located at the top of the Citadel's antenna transmitted onto the Island's television screens the gruesome image of this apocalyptic night. In the infernal center, where the explosions were concentrated, fiery sparks broke off from the main fire and then came together to resemble flaming trees towering toward the stars, composing a moving forest of light and horror. At the base of the fire, there were no longer any boats or any children. The sea itself was burning.

A terrible silence enveloped everyone on the Island. The adults stood before the screens, immobilized, stiff and tense, watching the flames. The children at the wharf dropped the raftlike barges they had been inflating and watched the nightmare on the wide screen. They trembled with fury and screamed in unison, "We must kill them! They must be killed!"

Den jumped onto a crate. "We must call for help! Call out to the world. Tell them to come and save us. We can tell them the truth about the treasure being hid from them here—the end of death. If they come, they will find immortality. The entire world will want to come if they know the truth. I'm going to call them with my radio transmitter. They'll come and save us."

He picked up an iron bar and brandished it in the direction of the door. "They'll try to keep us from doing this. We must get through!"

Den leaped to the ground and ran toward the door.

The boys and girls picked up whatever objects they could to use as weapons and ran behind him. As soon as he saw Den, the technician on guard in the radio room cut off the image of destruction outside the Island and began sending the scene on the wharf over all the circuits. Then the adults saw what was awaiting them in the next few minutes.

The Admiral wiped away the sweat running down his face. He didn't want to know about what he had just destroyed. Over the loudspeaker, he had heard the voices coming from the boats: "We are naked children."

But it wasn't his business to hear them or to understand what those words meant. It was his duty to execute orders. He had been sent here only to fulfill that mission.

His task was perhaps not terminated, since a last green point was moving across the radar screens. Navigating toward the south, it had stopped at the moment of the first explosions before reaching the buoys. It had turned back toward the Island, had stopped again and was now circling the Island in the opposite direction to the first row of warships and carriers.

Han had not been able to bring himself to follow the luminous arrow and reenter the Island. He felt—he knew—they should leave. He also knew that if he crossed beyond the buoys, he and his family would suffer the same fate as the other boats and their occupants. So, not knowing what to do, he had begun to sail around the Island, whose silhouette showed up clearly against the background of the fire.

It is said that a liberated pigeon flies three times around its village sky before flying away straight to the country awaiting it and into the range of hunters' rifles.

Chapter 39

Roland went to Bahanba's room and learned from his servant that Jeanne had come and gone. Going out into the streets again, he reeled under the shock of the images on the screens. He stopped short, horrified, realizing that everything they had tried to protect, all their hopes, their freedom and happiness were about to be destroyed. And suddenly, he knew where he would find Jeanne. He began to run, just at the moment that Den and the children left the wharf shouting and brandishing weapons.

The children poured out like a torrent of lava toward the center of the Island where the radio room was located. They broke everything in their way, destroyed everything they could lay their hands on as they passed. They went into the rooms, shattering the mirrors to make daggers out of the splinters of glass, snatching large knives from the kitchens. Behaving like a pack of wolves, they attacked every adult in their path. Terrified and overwhelmed, the adults barely tried to defend themselves, held back by the primal instinct that has always prevented parents from hurting their children. They fell to the ground, beaten unmercifully, slashed to pieces, and the horde of children trampled them and continued on, carried away by a collective fury and hate that defied all reason.

Mothers spoke over the television circuits, calling their children by name, begging them to become calm, to relinquish the idea of speaking over the radio to the rest of the world. The black Bishop appeared on the screens. He kneeled and cried out, "We're all guilty. We're all guilty. We beg you to forgive us. Be good and gentle like Jesus. Accept suffering and your brothers' sacrifices. Throw down your arms and pray with me!"

A spasm shook him, he twisted in agony as his stomach contracted and turned from the water he had drunk. No one had listened. The children could hear only the boiling of their blood and their own shouts. They rushed headlong toward the radio room, wounding or killing everyone who tried to get in their way.

Dr. Lins stood before them, his arms spread out, his heart overflowing with love and pity, crying, "My children, my children!"

A girl drove a splinter of glass into his mouth. They slit his throat and cut him to pieces, then they trampled his torn body, before running on.

Chapter 40

Jeanne saw the fire at sea and the revolt of the children, and all the violence became one with the absurdity and horror of her own situation. She followed the breeze which turned into a wind as it led her where she wanted to go, to the passageways closed by the iron grille. She looked for the grille under which the rails passed. A lock high on the ceiling, too high for the young children to reach, kept it closed. Jeanne raised her arm, turned the handle and entered a long oval room, windless and peaceful. She found Roland there waiting for her.

In the street leading to the radio room, some men

whom Galdos had assembled faced the assault led by Den and the older children. The adults had used work-benches and tables to form a barricade. It rose to the ceiling and echoed under the blows rained on it by the children.

The electronics specialists had feverishly searched for Den's radio set in order to destroy it. There were many finished and unfinished sets of all sizes in the workroom, and, not knowing which was Den's they began to break them all. But they were soon forced to stop and run to the barricade because it was beginning to give way.

The buffalo had drunk more than twenty quarts of water. Suddenly, pain tore at his stomach as though a thousand rats were gnawing away at it. It screamed out like a stampeding elephant and could be heard throughout the Island. For a moment, the children and adults stopped fighting to listen, but they then assumed that it was the sound of battle going on elsewhere. The children resumed their attack on the barricade, this time with an iron girder. The barricade began to weaken, and the men tried to pile up other material behind it. Maddened with pain, the buffalo lowered its enormous horns, broke through the stable door, charged into the chemistry laboratory and tore out of it covered with smoke and flames into the street. It trampled underfoot the wounded lying on the ground, tore up two foundations in a square, flattened a girl against an elevator door. Water began to stream down the streets. The wind grew stronger, clearing away the smoke from the burning laboratory.

Furious, the Admiral watched the small green spot that was soon going to complete its third turn around the Island. What were those idiots doing? Why didn't they turn back? But while he followed the boat, he could at least avoid thinking of those that were no longer afloat. The helicopters had been refilled with napalm and were flying around the Island outside the buoys in the same direction as Han's boat.

Han smiled at Annoa. She was seated next to him, their daughter on her knees. She seemed unafraid. She took his left hand in hers and put her forehead, her cheek and then her lips to the palm of his hand. Han looked at the instrument board and saw the arrow indicate that the entrance to the Island was to his left. South was therefore directly before him. He knew that he would soon have to decide what he must do.

Roland stood waiting for Jeanne in the middle of the room where the numerous small railway lines coming from the grille met at the far end of the room to form only two tracks. These tracks penetrated into a long, slightly slanted passageway. At the end of the passage was the fire.

Three of the secondary tracks were empty and three were occupied by long, low, tipping wagons. Animals were sleeping in the wagons. They were all kinds, all ages and all sizes—squirrels, birds, kittens, rabbits, guinea pigs, a deer with its fawn, and even flowers like violets, honeysuckle and primroses. A morsel of paradise innocently asleep, and excess of each species that the Island had to destroy in order to survive.

Spiraling curls of blue smoke finally dissolved, leaving behind an odor of vanilla and new-mown hay. When Jeanne inhaled the smoke, she felt her anguish leave her. Her body seemed to become lighter too. She saw an empty wagon move along the passage and enter one of the empty tracks, then stop. A full wagon began to glide down the passage. It was overflowing with enormous scarlet geraniums and yellow and blue birds. At the end of the passageway, the fire glowed. Roland came toward Jeanne slowly, holding out his hands.

On his screen, Frend saw the barricade where the radio room was located give way little by little under the savage attack of Den's troop. Despite the precise limitations of his mission, he thought there might be a possibility of saving what was left if he interfered. He spoke into the Island's microphone.

Han's boat ended its third turn around the Island and didn't begin a fourth. He blocked the wheel in the south-southeast direction and sat down beside Annoa. He took her hand, and she leaned her head on his shoulder.

The radar observer on the bridge transmitted the information that had been picked up.

"Subject is sailing south-southeast toward the first row of buoys."

The Admiral wiped his forehead nervously and gave the necessary orders.

The buffalo ripped off one of its horns against a concrete wall. Its head as well as its stomach now twisted with pain, and so it was doubly enraged. The wind carried off the smoke, birds, butterflies and fiery ashes. At the entrance to the street of the radio room, the buffalo saw moving targets and it charged. It trampled children to death, broke through the barricade and entered like a typhoon into the radio room, carrying with it Den, who was hanging onto its hairs blackened by fire and reddened with blood. Den fell to the ground, which was covered with water. He knew where to find his radio set, seized it and raced toward the antenna outlet. Galdos attacked him. A girl grabbed Galdos's arm from behind and bit his neck. He screamed and let Den go. The buffalo charged the children, the adults, the tables. Smoke filled the place, coming through the wind pipes with bouquets of butterflies in flames. Den branched his radio set onto the antenna. Some children made a circle around him, facing the adults, who this time attacked pitilessly, hitting out with tools and table legs. The buffalo passed by, tore apart some of the fighters and galloped out with a child impaled on its remaining red horn.

Frend's pleading voice could be heard all over the Island. "Stop fighting immediately. If you speak over the radio to the world, the Island will be destroyed. If you speak over the radio, the Island will be destroyed!"

Roland and Jeanne and all those not fighting heard him. But the noise of battle in the radio room made it impossible to hear Frend there. And even if Den had heard him, it wouldn't have made any difference.

The phrase "The Island will be destroyed" rebounded from the walls, echoed in the passageways and reached Roland and Jeanne.

"My love," Roland said, "time is going to end."

He gently took her in his arms. She stiffened, then closed her eyes and gave way. She stopped fighting, for there was neither time nor need left for battle. She no longer heard the roar of the fire or the words announcing the destruction of the Island, but only Roland's voice.

"Time no longer exists. Nothing separates us any longer. We have never really left each other."

It was true. The arms holding her were those of earlier years. They had never opened to let her go. Nothing had changed. Yesterday and today were one. Time had stopped.

"We're in the rue de Vaugirard, in our bed, you've returned from drinking a glass of water in the kitchen and have just awakened me."

She moved slightly, taking her exact place against him, the place that had been hers for eternity. They stood in each other's arms, in the middle of the room surrounded by birds and flowers and sleeping animals. Together, they were alone in the world.

Den succeeded in connecting his microphone. Protecting his transmitter with his body, disregarding the blows raining down on him, he cried, "Calling the world, calling the world. Help! Help!"

Frend realized that the time had come to complete his mission. He stopped speaking over the Island's microphone and again placed his hand on the yellow button of the small wireless box. He sent out in Morse code a brief signal of ultimate danger. He repeated it and continued to repeat it.

At the other end of the world, a hand reached out to an open case and pressed the button it contained.

Frend saw the first bulb in the case light up.

Han's boat passed beyond the first row of buoys. Over his receiving set came the usual warning. "Return or you'll be destroyed. Turn back!"

The boat continued in the south-southeast direction, toward the second row of buoys.

Frend's second bulb lit up.

Den cried into his transmitter, "I'm calling the world. Help! Help! I'm calling from the Island."

Frend didn't see the third bulb light. At the first second when his metal filament lamp began to heat up, the transmitter in the small closet sent the signal Frend had prepared toward the depths of the Island. With the swiftness of light, the signal reached the explosive Frend had placed on the atomic bomb that had been waiting at the deepest point inside the Island for seventeen years, in readiness for this moment.

Jeanne and Roland continued to embrace. They were standing at the top of the Arc de Triomphe, reunited under a blue sky, above the crowd, above the city, above the earth. Their end was instant and glorious as the heavens changed into a dazzling expanse of gold and radiant light.

The Island became transparent and illuminated the

fog for over a hundred miles, like a huge glowing lamp. A tempest of sound, light and heat waves erased the images from all the radar screens, killed radio reception so that the wires could only crackle with static. Helicopters, planes and ships suddenly became blind in the night as the mist glittered from the firey blaze. Bombs and napalm fell, flame-throwers spit out their red jets, ships collided and helicopters and planes collapsed into the burning sea.

A ham radio amateur in Rockhampton, Australia, heard an appeal for help in a language he could barely make out. It seemed to be a mixture of words from several languages. But he did understand the English word "Help, help!" repeated over and over again. The appeal was suddenly interrupted. He couldn't pinpoint where it had come from. He asked several of his correspondents throughout the world, but no one else had heard it.

The Island glowed through the mist for eleven days. At the end of two weeks, when the fog lifted, the once white cement of the Citadel was black.

The United States published a communiqué announcing that, in its pursuit of peaceful nuclear research, it had successfully exploded a controlled atomic charge in the depths of Islet 307, in the Aleutians. Everything had gone according to plan.

Chapter 41

In May, 1968, an exhausted, frightened, stupefied France waited for de Gaulle to speak out. The rest of the world was also curious to hear what he would have to say. The youth of the nation had set an entire section of Paris ablaze, and there were student uprisings throughout the rest of the country as well. Then they had demanded de Gaulle's resignation. Instead of answering, he had disappeared for two days. Later, it became public knowledge that he had gone to see General Massu, who was stationed in Germany, but no one ever really knew exactly why. Here is the real reason for that voyage.

When de Gaulle received from Colonel P. the phial that had been stolen from Khrushchev, he put it away in his personal safe at the Elysée, the Presidental palace. But during the years that followed, he became convinced that no safe at the Elysée was secure from secret-service agents. Nothing was ever taken, but he was certain they were inspected from time to time. On the first day the phial was in his possession, he had scratched out the label marked in three Cyrillic letters. Only Colonel P. had seen them, and he was now dead.

But that unmarked phial surely intrigued the agents who examined his papers from time to time, believing they left no traces. If one of them should ever take it, it would be a catastrophe, and de Gaulle feared an agent might be idiotic enough to do something like that. He changed the phial's hiding place several times and finally, as Khrushchev had done, began to carry it on his person. But this made him nervous for he was afraid of losing it.

He finally found a solution. Since he believed that Colonel Massu, being a soldier par excellence, was necessarily honest, tough and gifted with simplicity and clarity of mind, de Gaulle promoted him to the rank of general, gave him a command in Germany and handed the phial to him. He instructed General Massu that the entire army must be sacrificed to defend it, if necessary, and that the General should destroy it by fire before dying. Only then did de Gaulle sleep peacefully.

May, 1968, surprised him. "They" had profited from his absence by launching this collegiate revolution that might end in killing the France he had almost succeeded in rebuilding. Who were "they"? England perhaps, which had always hated France, and hated her more than ever now that she was recovering while England was going downhill. Or the United States, which did not want to accept the fact that France refused to bow down before the dollar. Unless it were the Chinese, with their religion of total and permanent revolution.

De Gaulle was weary and saw no practical solution. His mind was still clear enough, its lucidity at times even frightening. But at seventy-eight, after a relatively serious operation, his body tired easily, making it difficult for his mind to react quickly enough to counteract the young people in revolt and thus turn the tide in his favor. Then he remembered the phial and understood Kennedy.

If he took it, he would not become young, but he would at least remain a healthy and strong old man, his body's ills and weaknesses arrested. He would be able to act decisively and make France a great nation again. The problem of contagion could be handled later. First, it was imperative that he be in condition to do what had to be done.

He flew to Germany to see Massu and returned to Paris with the phial.

De Gaulle had announced that he would speak the evening of his return. His worried partisans and friends waited hopefully. His political adversaries and enemies waited angrily. The young, slightly astonished at having made so much noise and to such obvious effect, waited expectantly.

He called in his personal doctor, who remained in the next room. The television team had prepared everything. The President closeted himself alone in his office.

The case containing the phial was sitting on his desk. Standing erect, his hands clasped before him, he closed his eyes and prayed. "My God, do I have the right?"

He knew very well that he had the right. He had always known that he had the right. It was not that which made him hesitate.

"I'm an old man who has experienced so many hopes and disappointments. I have become an old man who doesn't want to die. They've already had enough of me. They'll hate me until one day they kill me. Should I make a decision that by all rights belongs to you alone? It's for France. Give me courage."

He had never lacked courage. Wasn't it perhaps better for France that he leave rather than make himself hated by his own people?

He allowed himself then to recall the peril he had consciously put from his mind—the possibility of contamination. If he drank the contents of the phial, he would become contagious. He then made his decision not to take the virus.

But what if Mao had taken it and was immortal? And what would happen if Mao's advisers and little by little all the Chinese people became infected?

De Gaulle opened his eyes and raised his head toward the ceiling. "In that case, it will be up to you to take care of it. To each his own task."

He sent his doctor away and went to meet the television team to deliver his message to the nation: "I shall stay on."

Though they couldn't know it, this meant that he had chosen to leave, like all other mortal men.

Chapter 42

No one knows what became of the phial de Gaulle had possessed. He didn't give it back to Massu. He didn't leave it at the Presidential palace. Did he destroy it? Did he take it with him to his private home at Colombey? Did he give it to a member of his family or hide it on his estate? Or, struck down by death unexpectedly, did he have time to dispose of it as he might have wished?

If he did not destroy it, somewhere in France there is a grain of immortality contained in a fragile glass that anything or anyone can unknowingly break.

Nixon tried in vain to discover whether the Navy had destroyed the eleventh small boat, the one which carried Han, Annoa and their infant daughter and which had been on the point of crossing beyond the second row of buoys. At the very moment when the Admiral's men were preparing to fire on it, the bomb had exploded, putting all the weapons and instruments out of commission.

Two helicopters had fallen and the sea had burned for hours at the spot where the boat should have been. When everything had cleared and the sea was again calm, nothing appeared on the radar screens. Air patrols searched far and wide but found nothing either.

Except that, coming out of the fog, there was a small white boat, resembling a Chinese junk, sailing south-southeast in the sun.